AUTUMN AND MAY

KD RYE

WOODLAWN PRESS

CHAPTER 1

SOMETIMES I WISH my lungs would stop working, my chest would stop moving, and my heart would stop pounding. Maybe then my body could relax, and I'd have a better night's sleep. There's so much commotion inside of me. The constant movement makes me shaky, and I feel like I'm going to crumble into sand. Like the dried up soil down by the river that the water doesn't really hit anymore. I want to lose myself in the tall grass and rest there for days, months, years. Is it so terrible to become a hermit? I wouldn't need much. I'd learn how to grow my own food, but I'd need to find clean water. I've been so thirsty lately. No matter how many cups of water I drink, I can't get the feeling of dryness out of my mouth. I need a break, some time to think about what's going on around me, a moment to find out where everyone is. Because it feels like I'm all alone. Even by the river, where the grass is tall, it's hard to take the silence.

"Autumn, are you almost done?" My manager, Greg Price, taps his foot impatiently behind me as I slowly sweep the main floor of Price's General Store. His white polo shirt hugs his skeleton body in a way that makes his veins stick out. Since it's the end of the night his usual streak of sweat runs down the side of his armpits. At least twice an hour he stands in front of the large industrial fan towards the back of the shop, but this does little to help.

Greg has been extra anal lately because we've been losing customers to the new Super Center 20 minutes away. He doesn't know how long the business will stay afloat and is desperate to come up with new ideas to attract customers. Besides the store-wide discount that's been going on for two months, Greg allowed the community skateboarders to spray paint a mural on the side of the building. Unfortunately, skateboarding doesn't guarantee any artistic skill, and the pubescent boys wrote something illegible in graffiti that looks like 'SKUTZ' with a giant dick running through the middle of it.

"Yeah, I'm just going to mop." I quicken my pace with the broom, and Greg goes into the back office while I finish up the cleaning. He's only a few years older than me, but is in charge because his grandfather used to own the business. I think he's trying to impress his dad or something. Whenever Greg's father comes in to check up on the place, Greg always tells him how great things are going. The guy just nods his head and talks on his phone the whole time. Poor Greg doesn't even have a chance.

From the back of the store I hear the front door open, and I walk up to the counter. We don't get a lot of customers at this time of night, especially on weekdays. I can make out the back of a woman's head poking up from the arts and crafts aisle. She turns around quickly and practically runs to the counter. It's Mrs. Irwin, the old crossing guard. She quit her job about three years ago. It's a terrible story. She called in sick to work one snowy day, but the school didn't bring anyone in to substitute her. When class got out and all those little kids started walking home, no one was there to help them. A six-year-old was hit by a car and became paralyzed. I don't think his family still lives in town.

"Did you find everything okay?" I ask, and Mrs. Irwin puts a handful of markers, construction paper, and a large poster board onto the counter. She gives me a small smile as she reaches a fidgety hand into her coat pocket and pulls out a crumpled $20 bill. She has a few kids of her own. I can't remember what grades they're in now, but they're young. This stuff is probably for a last minute school project. I watch Mrs. Irwin throw her bags into the car and drive away.

Even though the hours are long, my job at Price's isn't too bad. It mostly consists of helping customers, bagging, tidying up aisles, and cleaning 30 minutes before closing time. Usually I'm tired at the end of a shift, but lately the night sky is captivating. The cool wind blows through me like a wave hitting land, and I don't want to leave its comfort. I stay out hours into the night driving until my eyelids become too weak to defy gravity, and I have to go home.

I finish mopping, turn in my apron, grab my bag, and say goodbye to Greg, who nods vaguely to a calculator. I walk out to the parking lot and close my eyes. The breeze tickles the hair around my ears, and I pull my hood up. Tonight the wind is only a whisper, soft fingers running down my back. I sit inside my car with the door open for a few minutes, staring at the dried up field behind Price's. It's covered with half buried gravel and straw, but at night it looks kind of like a burned down cornfield. I like to squint my eyes and imagine that the figures are people watching me. I wave at them and the 'SKUTZ' before leaving the parking lot.

I drive slowly, taking the long route home. I've been having trouble sleeping lately, and driving is a little more relaxing than lying awake staring at the ceiling. Everything is dark, and only with my headlights can I make out the trees, the bushes, and the life that happens when no one's around. I guess this is the life that happens all the time, when everyone's around, but I'd like to think I notice it a little more closely than everyone else. It's a nice night. A fine night.

When I open the front door, the house is completely dark besides the TV light sneaking out from my mom's room. It's only 10 o' clock but she's probably been in bed since six. All she ever does now is sleep. She might leave her room when I'm at school or work, but if she does, it's only for a few minutes to get food or to use the bathroom. I know this because sometimes I'll skip out on school for a day, and when I do I barely see her. My dad tries to help me. We talk on the phone a couple of times a week and he's encouraging, but his presence would be better. He left a few months ago to give her space, but I think it's because he's fighting his own battles and there's not enough room in our house for a war.

I go into the kitchen and open the fridge only to find a few condiments, some old carrots, and half a loaf of bread. I should've gone shopping tonight. I'm starving and consider getting fast food, but the thought of eating factory made chicken nuggets makes me sick. I make some toast and tidy up a bit. Even though we barely eat, dishes still seem to pile up and food manages to spill on the counter. I have no idea where it comes from since I'm the only one who goes grocery shopping anymore, and I neglect those duties pretty often.

When the kitchen seems clean I knock on my mother's door. She doesn't answer, which isn't surprising. I open it a little, and am immediately overwhelmed by the smell of spoiled milk. There's a bowl of soggy Cheerios lying on her nightstand, probably from this morning or yesterday. How long has she been sleeping? I walk over to the bed and take the bowl.

"Mya?" my mom asks, sleepily, turning her head towards me.

"No, Mom, it's Autumn." I put the bowl down and sit on the edge of her bed.

"Autumn?" She blinks up at me, her face hard in concentration. "Honey, what are you doing?"

"I just got home from work. How are you feeling?" I put my hand on the side of her face and look down at her. She's become thin and pale. Her hair is stringy with grease and I have to fight the urge to pull my hand back when I see the collection of wax built up inside her ear.

"I'm just really tired," she mumbles, resting her head on her arm. I stare into her gray tinted eyes and trace the bags beneath them. How can someone who sleeps so much look so exhausted? I want to shake her awake. I want to yell at her. I want to tell her to move on, to get up and get on with her life. I also want to crawl into the bed next to her, wrap my arms around her middle, and bury my face in her back.

"Maybe tomorrow you can walk to the park and look for birds?" It's been a long time since my mother went bird watching. I can't even remember the last time I saw her binoculars. She used to love it though. Sometimes she'd bring Mya and me along with her. We'd sit on a bench eating sunflower seeds, staring up into the trees. I could never remember the names, but Mya would point to a starling and my mom would get so excited. Birds were never particularly interesting to me. I just liked sitting on the bench, between the two of them, eating sunflower seeds.

"No. I don't want to do that anymore." She rests her head back down on the pillow and closes her eyes. I take a deep breath. Who actually wants to do anything? Is that why people do stuff? Because they want to? I grab the bowl and walk towards the door.

"You really need to leave this room, Mom. It stinks in here." I shut the door and drop the bowl in the kitchen sink. I push down the guilt, rub my eyes, and pray that I don't hear her crying tonight.

I lie in my bed and look over my schoolwork. Senior year is pretty easy. I don't have a lot of homework, but I do need to finish reading *Beowulf* before tomorrow's English class. I try to concentrate, but my eyelids are heavy. Slowly everything warps into darkness, and I'm comforted by the weight of my exhaustion finally getting fed.

CHAPTER 2

My ALARM GOES off at six, and I hit snooze on the third buzz. My muscles are stiff from falling asleep in an odd position. I feel even more tired than I did last night, but somehow I manage to get out of bed and into the shower. The hot water feels good on my tight back and wakes me up enough to get dressed and find my backpack.

I look at the sofa and imagine my dad sitting there in his pajamas, watching the news. We usually talk in the mornings before I have to leave. I dial his number and listen to the ring. After a few seconds there's a click.

"Hello?" Hearing his voice is like biting into a lemon, but I push the feeling aside.

"Hey, Dad." There's a pause on the other line, and I imagine him smiling softly to himself.

"Hi, honey. How are you?" He sounds casual and distant, like he was in the middle of doing something important before I called. This is how it was when I used to call him after school, when I was a little girl, and he was still at work.

"Alright. I miss you. Mom misses you." I bite my lip and

stare up at the ceiling. He doesn't say anything. "How are you?" I ask.

"I'm okay. I miss you both. I've been keeping myself occupied with work. How's school?" He pauses for a second to cough heavily, something he can't help but do during conversations, a result of smoking for so many years.

"I just can't wait for it to be over." I sigh and rub a hand through damp hair.

"You're almost done kiddo. The next few months will go by so quick." I can hear in his voice a small smile. Maybe he's remembering his own last year of high school.

"Yeah, I guess you're right." I look down at my bare feet and rub them together.

"I'm proud of you, Autumn," he says, softly. I nod my head and take a deep breath.

"Thanks, Dad." I try to think of something else to say, mainly because I still want to hear him talk. He lets out a long sigh into the receiver and for a moment all I can hear is air passing.

"I'm sorry," he says, slowly. "I should be with you."

"It's okay. I know that you can't right now." This is always how our conversations end.

"How's your mom doing?" I don't feel like giving him an update, and I don't want to make him feel worse.

"I need to get ready for school," I tell him.

"Of course, have a good day. I love you." He coughs once more.

"Me too, Dad." I hang up the phone.

When Mya first got sick my dad was never around. He'd disappear in the afternoons for hours on end, and whenever I asked him where he was he'd simply say that he was driving. My mom confronted him about it one time, telling him he couldn't just run off when it got tough. His voice deepened, and his teeth jutted out, straining his anger. He yelled about it being better for all of us if he wasn't around. I think my mom flinched, even though she looked pissed. They let it drop though; Mya was napping on the couch.

I go to the bathroom and brush my hair. The mirrored image of myself is worse than I imagined. My brown eyes are big, wet, black holes, like something from a Tim Burton movie. I splash some water on my face and look back into the mirror. My eyebrows have grown wild. I haven't plucked them in months. I feel bad for neglecting myself. All of the stress has caused numerous wrinkles along my forehead and down the side of my mouth. My lips are blistered around the corners, and my hair has so many split ends it's like the softer end of straw. I finish washing my face and grab my bag off of the bed. Mya used to do my make-up in the mornings before school when she was in recovery. It gave her something to do, and I looked presentable enough for people to feel welcomed to talk to me.

I walk out the back door and step into my car when I realize my mother won't have anything to eat while I'm away. I quickly go to The Bagel Store. It's not the heartiest breakfast, but it's better than fast food. I hate that I have to go out of my way for my mother like this, but it's not like I can just let the woman starve herself to death. The lady at the drive-through smiles at me and asks for my order. I pay for the bagels and leave them on the kitchen table. If she wants to eat, she'll have to get up and get the food herself. I worry she won't even do that much.

I make it to school in time to go to my locker before the bell rings. As I open my bag I realize that, in my hurry to take care of my mother, I've forgotten to get myself something to eat for lunch. I'm also out of cash, and the lunch ladies don't accept credit cards. Perfect. I feel like crying, but instead take some deep breaths. I've been letting the exhaustion get to me.

"Excuse me?" I feel a tap on my shoulder and turn around. A girl close to my height with shockingly blue eyes stares back at me. We look at each other for a moment, and I realize that I'm gawking with my mouth hung open, like a social misfit.

"I'm sorry for bothering you, but I'm new here and a bit lost. Could you tell me where room 157 is?" She talks quickly and smiles nervously at me. A magenta scarf is wrapped loosely around her neck that holds a gothic-like pattern with gray accents. It looks soft, like it's made from silk. When she takes it off the whole thing unfolds. The design is actually an abstract picture of the night sky. I smile back and try to make myself appear normal.

"Sure, I can take you there if you want." I swallow hard because it's been awhile since my last conversation with someone who wasn't a teacher.

"You don't have to do that. I don't want to take you out of your way." Her voice is naturally loud, and when she talks the corners of her mouth curl up. She seems happy and the general nature of the expression strikes me.

"I actually have class there too, so it wouldn't really be out of my way." I put my coat in my locker and pull out a few books in exchange. "You must be a senior then?" I ask her. "Only seniors can take Economics."

"Yeah, I guess that's so." She makes a crooked smile. "They just gave me the schedule. I didn't get to pick any of the classes."

"There's not much of a selection anyway," I tell her. "You're not missing out on anything." The bell rings, and I jump. "Shit! We're late for class." I throw my backpack around my shoulders and start walking down the hall. We pace silently together but then slow down.

"I'm May, by the way." She holds out her hand.

"Autumn." I reach over and shake it. She looks at me again, and I can't get over how blue her eyes are.

"Your eyes are stunning," I say before thinking about my words. May laughs and looks away.

"Thank you. I get them from my father." She seems flattered, so I try not to feel too embarrassed. She smiles at me, her lips coiled upward, and this time I notice the freckles surrounding her nose. She scratches them with the tip of her deep lavender painted fingernail. "So do you live in town?"

"Yeah, well, sort of. I'm on Prospect, it's a little towards the outskirts, but still within walking distance to everything, not like one of the farm houses. Where do you live?" I ask. She stops for a moment and puts her hand to her chin.

"Oh, wow, this is embarrassing. I don't exactly remember. We just moved in a few days ago. I know that there's a laundry mat down the block."

"Maple Ave.?"

"Yes, Maple Avenue. I really have to remember that."

"Here's the classroom." I open the door to find my peers talking to one another. Mr. Busman hasn't begun his lecture yet. I sigh in relief. What a perfect day to be late. I walk up to the teacher's desk where a balding old man sits hunched over a newspaper, grumbling not so quietly to himself.

"Mr. Busman?" I say, softly at first, but he doesn't hear me. "Mr. Busman," I yell.

"What?" He looks up quicker than I thought his old bones could allow and I try not to jolt back. "Autumn, can you believe this?" He lifts up the newspaper, smacks it with a flick of his wrist, and jumps to the front of the class.

"Let's just go sit down," I whisper as Mr. Busman spews information about surplus and deficits.

I lead May to the two empty seats in the back of the room. The class gives us subtle glances. I can feel their eyes looking us over, well, probably May more so than me. It must be pretty uncomfortable to know that a group of students are judging you solely on your appearance. We sit down, and I take in her outfit for the first time myself. A dark green three-quarter sleeve shirt, a pair of dark jeans, and flats. It doesn't give me any implications about her. The most unique item she had on was the scarf. That thing could be from Italy, it's so beautiful. Either way she's dressed better than me. I'm still wearing sweaters from three years ago and my jeans are at least a size too big. I haven't bought anything new since Mya was alive.

"I'm handing out a packet due at the end of class. You can work in pairs, but no excessive talking. Everything you read will be on the test next week, so pay close attention." Mr. Busman gives us each a five-page packet, and May moves her desk closer to mine. Her long hair brushes against the side of my face as she leans forward and flips through the pages of our class work. I watch as she skims the questions and smiles to herself.

The period goes by slowly. We finish everything on time, and I hand in the packet. Before the bell rings we compare schedules and realize we don't have another class together until sixth period lunch and then English right after. I point May to her next class and wish her luck. As I walk into advanced art I wonder what it's like to move to a different school, what it'd be like to live somewhere else. I think a change would be nice, a chance to start something new. I've lived in this same town my whole life, and I've always been pretty content. I should ask May where she moved here from.

The rest of my day goes by in a daze, like it always does. It's hard to keep track of everything. Sometimes I even forget what room I'm supposed to go to in between classes, but I can tell from my stomach grumbling that I should be in lunch right now. I walk over to my regular lunch table where a few of my old friends sit. We don't talk much anymore, but they're nice enough to let me sit at the end of their table. It's been hard trying to keep friends after everything that's happened.

"Autumn." I look up and May is almost yelling my name. "You space out a lot, huh?" she asks.

"It's a bad habit." I blink rapidly and stare up at her across the table.

"Do you mind if I sit with you?" May asks, nervously twisting her fingers together. I don't understand why she'd want to, but I'm happy that she does.

"Not at all. No one else is going to sit there." May plops down across from me. Everyone at the table glances over at us. They wait a minute, like I'm going to say something to them, and then continue talking to each other.

"You don't eat lunch?" May asks, staring at the empty space in front of me while taking out her brown paper bag.

"Oh no, I usually do. I just didn't pack one today." I feel stupid not doing anything. I don't want to make things awkward by watching her eat, so I open my backpack and take out my sketchbook.

"Are you hungry? You can have half of my sandwich." She takes out a plastic knife and cuts her sandwich in half.

"No that's okay. I had a big breakfast anyway." I wave her hand away, and she slowly draws it back, unsure how persistent she should be. I give her a friendly smile to assure her that I'll be fine. She takes a bite of her sandwich, and I flip open my sketchbook.

"Do you draw?" May asks, stretching her neck over the table. "Can I look?" She points to the book. I don't usually show people my work, but there's something about May that makes me feel comfortable.

"Alright." I close the book and pass it over to her. "They're not that good though." I feel my cheeks turn to hot coals as a light shade of scarlet washes over me. Watching May stare down at the most personal part of me makes me more self-conscious than I thought it would. My fingers twitch under the table. May slowly flips through the pages, looking at each sketch carefully.

"You don't think that you're good?" she asks, keeping her eyes on my drawings.

"It's just something I do in my free time. I know that I'm still an amateur. You don't have to lie." I wave my hand at the book, like I'm ready to disown it with a simple gesture, when it's really one of my most valuable possessions. May cradles the book like a newborn in her arms, and the image relaxes me.

"You shouldn't be so hard on yourself. They're very unique. My mom's an artist too. I think she'd really like these." May looks up at me and smiles.

"I'm not an artist, but thank you," I say. May closes the sketchbook and gives it back to me. I put it in my backpack. "What kind of art does your mom do?"

"She enjoys everything—painting, sculpting, and drawing. She's even done portraits in England for the royal family." May enthusiastically leans forward across the table, her eyes wide at her mother's accomplishments. "That's why we travel so much. She likes to go everywhere and capture everything," May says in a mocking tone, nodding her head in a know-it-all manner.

"How far have you traveled?" I ask, eagerly.

"Well, I was born in Italy where my parents raised me for a few years. However, I don't speak the language. We traveled along Europe, and my mom fell in love with Paris, so we lived there for a while. My dad was finally able to drag her away to Belgium and then Denmark. I wanted to go to Ireland, but we were never able to live there. My parents wanted me to go to high school in America and my mom thinks this town is beautiful. So, here we are, and everyone's happy." May stops moving her hands and folds them in her lap.

"Do you only speak English?"

"For the most part, but I can understand Italian and a little French."

"I'm surprised you don't have an accent."

"I used to." May shrugs her shoulders. "But I like to adapt to the way the majority of people enunciate. It makes it easier to fit in."

"That's understandable." Accents have always seemed unique and beautiful to me. I don't really see why someone would want to change that. "I bet you can do some pretty good impressions though," I tell her. She lifts an eyebrow and smiles.

"Alright, mate, I'll give a bloody British accent," she says, and I laugh.

"That's really good." May takes a bite of her sandwich. We sit together quietly. The sound of lunchroom chaos comes in loud bursts, like a huge drum being smashed, adolescent conversation filling every inch of the room. I barely realize that May has started a conversation again. "So have you lived here your whole life?"

"Yeah." I roll my eyes. "I've lived in the same house, on the same street, in the same town since birth. Compared to you I probably seem pretty boring." I smirk, half joking, but well aware that it's likely true.

"Actually I think it must be nice to have a home that's familiar to you. I've always wished for something permanent, something consistent." I understand that type of desire, the need for stability, for a house that feels like a home.

"So is this a nice town compared to others?" I ask, although I'm sure it's nothing compared to Venice or Paris.

"It's very pretty, and I love how the river runs alongside everything. The trees are so colorful and everything seems so fresh. My mom's crazy for it. She wants to paint all of it."

I want to ask May what it's like to have a mother who's an artist, but the bell rings, and we have to go to English. As we enter the classroom I realize that I forgot all about *Beowulf* and mentally hit myself in the head. There's supposed to be a quiz today, and I barely read the text. I sit down, and May follows, taking the desk next to me.

"We have a quiz today on *Beowulf*," I tell her, sinking into my seat.

"Isn't that a poem?" May asks. "I think I've read parts of it."

"Yeah, it's an epic."

Ms. Rogan, the English teacher, starts the class by discussing college resumes and applications. I haven't even begun to think about schools or majors or higher education. It doesn't even seem like a possibility. I'm just trying to make it to graduation. Ms. Rogan starts to hand out the quizzes. I take one and pass the pile to the seat behind me. It's multiple-choice, so it shouldn't be too hard to guess the right answers. Even if I fail it's not going to matter.

After everyone finishes the quiz we spend the rest of the period debating whether or not old English literature is important for us to know before going to college. After 10 minutes the debate branches off into separate conversations, and everyone is soon talking about sports and parties. Ms. Rogan sits at her desk to grade papers. May touches my shoulder, and I turn to face her.

"I know we only just met today, but I was wondering if you could show me around town after school, if you aren't too busy. I don't really know my way around yet, and it's a beautiful afternoon." May's eyes dart around the room nervously, and she bites her bottom lip. I don't work on Fridays, and it'd probably only take an hour to show her the whole town. It'd also be a nice change to spend an afternoon with someone. I can't remember the last time I did anything with a friend.

"I'd love to show you around. I mean I do know this place fairly well," I say, and May's face lights up. She seems so alive, so happy with life. I like it. "I do need to go grocery shopping though. Do you mind if we make a pit stop first?"

"Not at all. I guess I'll need to know where the grocery store is anyway." May smiles, and the bell rings. We each have one more class and agree to meet up in the back parking lot after school. Math Finance drags on, and I find myself eyeing the clock every two minutes. I'm excited and even a little nervous about hanging out with May. I don't know why. I'm just being friendly towards a new student. I wait patiently until the last bell of the day rings.

I find May standing a couple of cars down from me and call out her name. She looks around and waves when she sees me. She hops in the front seat, and I slowly back out.

"So is this your car?" May asks, looking around the old Chevy.

"No, it's my mom's, but she doesn't drive it anymore," I say, turning onto the main street. The convenient thing about small towns is that there's usually one long road that runs through the center, connecting everything.

"Did she get a new one?" May cracks her window open and closes her eyes as the wind blows in her face.

"No, she just stopped driving," I say. "Towards the left here is Price's General Store, where you'll find school supplies, Butterfinger bars, and on most days, me."

"You work there?"

"Yup, and just a little further is one of the three gas stations in this town. Next to that is Nan's Fish Fry, and across the street is a pizza place that's pretty good." I drive slowly since no one's behind me and so May can get a good look at everything. "Up the road just a little further is our destination—the supermarket." I pull in and park the car. May jumps out and looks around at all the shopping carts lying in the parking lot, plastic bags flying through the air, and birds too weak to soar. She must think that America is such a dump compared to everywhere else she's been. The litter and pollution is enough to kill someone.

"Thanks for bringing me along. It means a lot to me," May says as we walk into the grocery store.

"No problem, it's kind of nice showing you around. Gives me a sense of purpose," I say, jokingly. As we walk down the aisles, May talks about what it's like in France and the types of food other countries eat. It's easy to get wrapped up in her stories. I imagine myself in a boat floating through Venice or walking the cold English streets. Time passes quickly. Before I know it we're back in my car, and I'm showing May the town park, the community center, and the nursing home.

"Do you need to be home at a certain time?" May asks, concerned. It's getting dark, and I should get the groceries home before the milk spoils.

"No, but it is late. Should I just drop you off at your

house?" I'm already close to Maple Ave. It's a quarter of a mile up the road.

"That'd be great, if you don't mind."

"Not at all, what number are you?" Maple Ave. is actually a dead-end road with trees lined on each side. Most of the leaves already lie on the ground in front of the old Victorian houses.

"38, a little way down on the right." May points to a creamy white colored building with big, open windows. I pull up in front of it and put the car in park.

"It's a beautiful house," I tell her.

"Thanks, you'll have to come over sometime so I can give you a tour. I'm sure my mom will want to meet my new artist friend." May flashes me a wide smile. "Thanks for showing me around today. It was really nice of you." She looks at me sincerely and gives me a hug goodbye before getting out of the car. I watch her walk up the path to her house and then drive away. The ride is only a few minutes from May's house to mine. When I pull in my drive-way all the events from this morning, from last week, from my whole life fly back to me, and I remember who I am. I'm not a European traveler, and I don't have a famous artist as a mother. My mom is probably in bed right now trying not to think about her life.

I take the grocery bags from my car and bring them into the kitchen. The house seems quieter than usual. I don't hear the low hum of my mom's TV coming from her bedroom. I call out her name, but she doesn't answer. I run to her room and throw open the door. She isn't in her bed.

"Mom?" I yell, running through the house. Panic washes over me, and I'm terrified until I walk into the living room and find her lying on the couch, asleep. There's a half-eaten bagel on the coffee table, and on the floor next to the couch is an old family album. Oh Mom, why were you looking through this? I pick it up and hide it behind the bookshelf. Sometimes it's almost like she tries to be depressed.

"Mom?" I shake her a little harder than I mean to. She stirs and rolls over.

"Mya?" I move her head so she's looking at me, and force her eyes open.

"No, it's Autumn. What are you doing?" I look at her hard, but she just stares up at me blankly, like I'm a stranger.

"I was just resting. How was school?" She sits up, and I take in her full appearance. Her hair is stringy with sweat and grease, and she's wearing an old, stained white shirt with a pair of sweat pants.

"You need to take a shower." I pull her arm, and she pushes me away.

"You don't tell me what to do. Who do you think you are?" Her face is a strange mixture of anger, exhaustion, and confusion. I barely recognize her. There's no way this woman gave birth to me. My mother never kept herself like this.

"Do what you want. I just thought that you needed help getting yourself cleaned up." I stand up and look down at her like she's some sort of foreign object. Her body is so small. I put my hand on her shoulder, and she shudders at the contact. "It'll make you feel better and you can rest in the tub," I say through gritted teeth, my eyes pleading. She looks away from me and tries to run her fingers through her hair. They get tangled in the grease knots, and she has to yank her hand free mid-swipe. She nods her head and follows me into the bathroom. I get the bath ready and have her pick out new clothes to wear. She says nothing the whole time. While she's in the tub I sit on the toilet seat and wait.

"It's supposed to be warmer outside tomorrow, a good day to go out," I say, but she doesn't respond. "I went grocery shopping today, so there's plenty of food in the fridge. I'll make you a salad or a sandwich after this."

"I'm not hungry." She doesn't look at me. She just stares into the water.

"You have to eat something tonight. You don't look healthy. You look sick."

"Maybe I am sick," she snaps.

"Well, if you want to get better you have to start taking care of yourself. You're not eating, you don't leave the house, and all you do is sleep. Is that the kind of life you want?" I'm getting angry with her, and my voice rises.

"You don't understand."

"I don't understand?" I ask in disbelief. "I don't understand what? Loss? Losing someone close? Being alone? Feeling cut off from the rest of the world? Tell me exactly what it is that I don't understand." I'm practically yelling at her, but I don't care. She just sits there not looking at me, wrapped up in her own self. I leave the bathroom and stomp down the hall into my bedroom.

I listen to my mom get out of the tub. I imagine her looking at herself in the bathroom mirror. I imagine her lightly touching the bags under her eyes and staring at herself in disbelief. I imagine her suddenly realizing what a mess she's become; she quickly turns around and runs to my room, flinging the door open. I look up confused, but really, I knew she'd come around. She immediately apologizes and promises to change. She tells me that from now on it'll be different. Tomorrow, she'll see if her old job will take her back. She'll take care of everything. Then I tell her about Dad, and she wraps her arms around me while I cry. She rubs my back and tells me that everything will be okay. That we'll make it through this together.

Mom walks out of the bathroom, past my room, down the

stairs, and into the kitchen. It's quiet for a few minutes, and I get nervous, wondering what she's doing. The fridge opens, and I can hear her moving things around. She takes something out of the cabinet—a plate maybe? She pulls out one of the chairs from beneath the table and sits down. She's eating. It's a start.

CHAPTER 3

ON SATURDAYS, I work from eight to four, so I have to wake up early to get ready. I look outside my bedroom window and see a little boy riding a tricycle while a woman watches, the morning sun—a penny floating in the sea—and Mrs. Moore, our next door neighbor, picking the paper up off of her lawn. It's going to be a warm day for October.

I don't know if I should call my dad or not. It's draining talking to him when his absence is so much louder than his presence ever was. I grab the phone and call him anyway. It rings, but he doesn't pick up. It's a little unusual; he always answers the phone for our morning conversations. It's not uncommon for him to bring his work home on the weekend though. I leave the phone and walk down the hall to shower.

I turn the water on extra hot and use the extension to beat the water into my back. I roll my shoulders back and forth to loosen the muscles. I was told by a palm reader once that I carry all of my stress on my back. She said that she could see it weighing down on me. I didn't let her look at my hand.

There's a knock on the bathroom door, and it opens without waiting for an answer. I hear someone sit on the toilet with a grunt and know it's my mother. I wait, but she doesn't say anything. Through the opening of the curtain I look at her. The sun comes through the window in speckles, leaving shadows of leaves on the wall across from the tub. I follow my mother's gaze and I can see that this is what she is staring at. The wind blows the shadows back and forth, and she follows it. Can she see the beauty like I do? Is she able to?

She stands up, and I close the curtain. Once she leaves the bathroom I turn off the water and step out of the shower. I touch the shadows on the wall and look out the window. Every morning at this time I bet these are here. I wrap my towel around myself and run into my bedroom, quickly retrieving a pencil. I trace the leaves onto the wall and leave the pencil on the counter. It's getting late, so I dress quickly, grab my bag, and run to my car. The sun is misleading, and the fall wind creates an unexpected chill. I turn on my car, but don't start driving yet. I flip open the mirror above my seat and look at myself. I purse my lips, narrow my eyes, and smile. Not big or bright, but just enough to get me through the day.

At Price's I'm able to let my mind wander between the boxes of old action figures and coloring books. When Mya first got sick she had a lot of trouble eating. She said that the smell and taste of everything had multiplied. The hospital food was especially hard to choke down because it wasn't very good in the first place. Our father usually ate her lunches since she wouldn't, and it's not like he had any extra money to go out and buy himself anything. But sometimes Mya did get hungry, and she'd order the blandest thing on the menu, usually mashed potatoes. When he'd take over our mother's shift at the hospital and see a little plate of watery potatoes in front of him he'd throw a fit, asking Mya how this was going to feed a grown man.

It's memories like these that conflict my love towards him. I want him to come back home, but sometimes I feel like it may be better that he's gone. Mya's death distraught my parents in different ways. My father was able to hide it better than my mother, but the raw emotion would seep out. At night, he'd sit in the dark in the living room and scream very, very quietly. I saw him like that once, and it terrified the hell out of me.

Towards the end of my shift, Kelvin, another Price's employee, arrives and stands around while I organize behind the counter. He graduated a few years ago and takes classes at a two-year school. He has a lot of spare time. Even when he's not on the clock he'll come into work to hang out with Greg. It's incredibly annoying.

"Something on your mind, Autumn? You look distracted." He takes a step closer to me, and I immediately move over. He's the kind of guy who always smells like ointment or some kind of weird lotion. As he opens his mouth I stare in disgust at the yellow plaque that's taken over his teeth. You can't even see the enamel anymore. His face is covered in white puss—mountains of red fury.

"I'm just tired," I tell him and begin to stack cigarettes. He grabs a blue pen on the counter and uses it to scratch at his thick, greasy black hair. I'll have to remember never to touch it again.

"Yeah, I know what you mean. I was up late last night watching movies." He puts the end of the pen deep into his mouth and chews on it. I'll have to throw it out when he's not looking.

"That's what you do every night." I know that watching 'movies' actually means watching porn. Supposedly it's one of Kelvin's favorite activities. It's probably the reason why he's on his sixth semester at a two-year college. I've overheard him and Greg talking about his extensive collection. He lends them to Greg to make up for his tardiness.

"It helps me fall sleep." Kelvin shrugs his shoulders and continues to chew on the pen. I break up the empty cardboard boxes that the cigarettes come in and bring them to the back of the store. In the hallway, leading to the rear door where the dumpsters are, is a mess of empty beer bottles that customers bring back for redemption, and ripped up boxes. I open the door to fresh, fall air and the sky, dark in thunder. I have to suppress the urge to run through the field and down to the river. Instead, I quickly throw the boxes in the recycling bin, put the bottles in the beer shed, and stand with my arms outstretched so that the breeze washes over me, a shower of wind to help wipe the sweat away. The sun starts to fall.

It's amazing how good life can feel in this way, even after everything. It almost seems like I shouldn't be allowed to enjoy it, and part of me doesn't want to. I know I should just accept the pain, the death, and move on, but it's so hard to see past it. How do you step onto the beach when you know that your ship is sinking to the bottom of the ocean?

When I go inside Kelvin is ringing up a customer at the counter. I watch in amazement as he passes her the blue pen from behind his ear and she, without hesitation, grabs it from his long dirty fingernails and signs the receipt. I shiver and look for Greg to tell him that my shift is over. I find him by a pile of weekend newspapers, taking inventory. He looks at his watch and waves me away before I even say a word.

When I get home my mom is sitting at the kitchen table with a cup of tea in front of her. She's staring out the window with a look of confusion plastered on her worn out face. I drop my bag onto the table.

"What are you looking at?" I put my hands on her cup to

see if it's still warm, and it is. She stares at me, surprised, like she just now realized I'm in the kitchen with her.

"Would you like a cup?" She walks to the stove, picks up the kettle, and carefully pours the warm liquid into a mug. She's dressed in a pair of jeans and a v-cut long sleeve shirt. Her soft auburn hair is in a ponytail. She smiles kindly at me while she hands me the tea. I stare at her, stunned.

"Thanks," I mumble, still watching her. She sits back down across from me. "Are you okay?" I ask. My mother's lips twitch slightly.

"I couldn't find the photo album today." She sighs and puts her hands under her chin like she's holding her head up. "Do you know where it is?" I look down into the light brown water and blow into it. I don't know if the album makes her worse or not. I don't know if staring at old memories will help her let go of the past. Either way, I don't want her to have it.

"No, have you checked the bookshelf?" I take a sip of tea and she looks up at me.

"Of course I've checked the bookshelf." Mom slams her hands down on the kitchen table and stands up quickly. She walks out of the room and opens the closet door, taking out her coat. I rush to get up and follow her.

"Where are you going?" I ask nervously. She puts on a pair of old sneakers and looks up at me.

"Can I have my keys?" She holds out her hand. I've kept too much from her already today. I give her the keys.

"I'm going with you." She says nothing, but I follow her out the door. I think back to all the times when I wished that she'd leave the house. All those times I imagined her pulling out of the driveway on her way to work. She puts the car in drive, and I ask her again where we're going.

"Autumn." She stares at me strangely, like she's looking

at something that's not quite there, desperation dripping from her chin. "I need to see Mya."

We pull into the cemetery and search for Mya. Looking at all the other graves decorated with flowers, I wish I brought something for her. My mom sits in front of the stone that reads Mya's name and runs her fingers over the engraved words. *Loving sister, daughter, and friend.* I wait as she cries, as she hits the ground with her fists, as she asks God why this happened. I watch as my mother stands up, wipes the tears from her cheeks, and walks to the car. I kneel down in front of my big sister's grave.

I don't have anything to say, but I wish that Mya could talk to me. I want to hear her voice. I want her to tell me that everything will be okay, but the only thing I hear is the wind blowing and the car starting. I stand up and look over at my mother who sits in the driver's seat. Slowly, I walk away from Mya, leaving her in this cold, dark graveyard. Each step makes my stomach sink, but I grind my teeth and continue moving. When I get into the car my mom doesn't say anything. She's silent the whole ride home and doesn't answer when I ask if she's alright. She opens the front door and goes straight to her bedroom. I know that she'll stay there for the rest of the night.

I walk into the kitchen and sit at the table. Everything is dark and quiet. I lean my head into my hands and try not to think. I try to suppress the rising sickness that shakes my bones. One time when Mya was in remission, we were running outside along the cross country track at school. It was an early-November afternoon, and Mya had to wear her winter coat since she got cold easily. Her skin was so thin. Near the end of our run Mya tripped over a root and fell into a tree. Her head hit the trunk, and she scraped her knee against the ground. She sat there for a long time, crying because her body was so breakable. She thought that after all of the fighting, all of the struggling, she'd die because of a tree. I'd never seen her face like that before. When I think about life in these regards I find it hard to blame my mother for her withdrawal from the world. If I could, I probably would too, but I know Mya would've hated that.

CHAPTER 4

I AWAKE to big droplets of rain pounding—like bullets hitting steel—at the window above my desk. I rub my eyes and kick the covers off my body. What an appropriate start to a Sunday morning. I vaguely remember waking up in the kitchen and walking upstairs to my bedroom. I drifted from old memories to nightmares for the rest of the night until I found solace when the sun was just rising. I stand up and saunter over to the window. There are puddles in the street and in the ditches on our front lawn. The fall leaves are now clenched to the grass in a wet embrace, and it's going to be twice as hard to rake them up. I look closely outside and notice someone walking around holding an umbrella. She's wearing a black rain jacket with the hood pulled over her face. The rain hits her hard, and I know she must be soaked. Her head whips back and forth looking at each house. When she turns to me I recognize her immediately. May's magenta scarf wraps tightly around the bottom of her face, and if I squint, I can make out the blue in her eyes. I run down the stairs and swing open the front door.

"May," I yell out, but she doesn't hear me. "May," I yell

again, and run over to her. She turns around and pulls the scarf below her mouth.

"Hey." She waves her arm.

"Are you lost?" I ask, smiling. "You shouldn't be out in this mess." I scold her and peel the wet hair away from her forehead. She doesn't pull away from the contact like I would've.

"I know, but it started rather suddenly. I was going for a walk, thinking that maybe you'd join me, and it started pouring." She laughs, and I can't help but smile. "I remembered the name of your street, but I don't believe you ever told me the number, so I was kind of winging it." She looks unsure of herself, and even though the situation strikes me as a bit strange, I don't want her to feel uncomfortable.

"I live right here." I point to my house even though we're standing in the front lawn. A shiver runs down my spine, and I remember that I'm barefoot and in my pajamas. "Would you like to come in?" I hunch over and draw my elbows closer into my ribs. May puts her hands over my shoulders and starts to brush away the wetness.

"I do want to get out of the rain, but you probably don't need any unexpected visitors." May looks down at my feet and starts to rub my shoulders harder, pushing me closer to her. I start to feel warm. It's been awhile since we've had any guests, expected or not, and I'm filled with anxiety at the thought of letting someone in. After everything, our house has been empty for so long. I clench my teeth together and look into May's watery, clear eyes.

"I think an unexpected visitor might be exactly what I need." We walk to the front door, and I open it for her. She takes off her coat, careful not to let too much water drip on the floor. I scratch my feet against the carpet and shake my arms out.

"Let me get us both a towel." I go down the hall to the closet next to my parent's bedroom. I pull out two towels and listen carefully to see if there's any noise coming from the room, but it just sounds like the TV is on low.

I find May standing in the living room, looking at the pictures on the wall. Her head is arched slightly, and I watch as her fingers lace in between her scarf's loose strings, unraveling it into a rope of silk. I find myself hanging onto the fabric as it falls away, revealing a slender, yet masculine neck. I walk behind her and drape the towel over her shoulders. She jumps forward, startled, and quickly turns around.

"Thank you." She laughs, drying off her face and hair. I pull my own towel around my chest.

"Are you hungry or thirsty?" I ask, and she follows me into the kitchen.

"No, I'm good." She sits on the stool next to the counter. I take out a cup and hold it under the tap. May looks around the kitchen while brushing wet hair out of her face. There's something so serene about her presence. It's kind of like lying in a nice, warm bed. That safety you feel when you're wrapped tightly in a blanket, and you can hear the wind pushing against the window.

"How has your weekend been so far?" I ask.

"Slow. My parents are the worst at unpacking. I had to sneak away this morning." May takes off the towel.

"Are they particular or something?" I take a sip of water and lean my body onto the counter across from her.

"The exact opposite. They get distracted every two minutes. That's the trouble of living with artists." May smiles to herself but then quickly shakes her head. "Not that all artists are unfocused. I'm sure that you're way more grounded."

"Don't worry, I hardly consider myself an artist, and I'm probably just as unstable." I give May a small smile.

"Just modest is all." May looks around the kitchen. "I've noticed that none of your work is hanging up."

The observation surprises me. "I've never thought to display it."

"I'd love to see it." May lifts her eyebrows up and flashes me another smile. I look down at the counter and collect the scattered crumbs into a neat pile. A loud thump emerges from my mother's room. I shake my hands out and return May's smile. She doesn't question the noise.

"Come, I'll show you where I keep my paintings." I walk to the other side of the counter, and May stands up from her stool. She touches my hand and gives it a small squeeze before wrapping her towel tighter to her chest. She follows me up the stairs quietly.

"Whose room is this?" May stops in front of the room diagonal from mine. The door is open slightly, and I can make out Mya's unmade bed and dresser.

"It was my sister's," I say quietly.

"Well, she has a nice taste in bands." May nods to the poster on Mya's wall.

"Yeah, I think so too." I remember when Mya and I spent hours during the summer sitting on lawn chairs, listening to the radio, and calling in for every contest to try to win concert tickets. We were always too slow, but the attempt was fun.

I shut the door to Mya's room, not wanting to look at her old things anymore. May doesn't say anything. She just smiles softly and follows me to my own room. I turn on the light and the TV. It's already dark and dreary enough in my room, and the rain doesn't help. May looks at all the paintings hanging on my wall.

"You really should show my mother your drawings. She'd

love you," May says, holding up a water color of a woman looking out a window, a painting that I was going to give my mother before Mya died. "How long have you been doing this for?"

"What? Painting?" I ask, shaking the wetness from my hair.

"You know, creating, painting, and giving meaning to the world." She tosses her hands in the air to emphasize each word dramatically.

"I don't think I give much meaning to anything. I keep telling you, I'm just an amateur." I sit down on the bed, and she looks at the painting for a moment longer.

"Amateur or not, you definitely have talent." May rests the canvas back against the wall and sits next to me. Another shiver runs down my spine, and I pull the blanket over my shoulders. May slides closer to me and pulls the other corner over herself as well. The closeness of her body next to mine warms me more than the blanket ever could, and I relax in the heat.

"So where are your parents? Do they work on the weekends or something?"

I shake my head at the question. "They're separated. My dad doesn't live here, and my mom," I breathe the words out. "Is downstairs sleeping," It's hard to speak this reality aloud. My head feels heavy, and I blink a couple of times, trying to shake myself out of it.

"How long ago did it happen?" May asks, eyeing the pictures resting along the walls.

"About three months." The memory of my mom's wails throughout the house on the night my dad left attempts to enter my mind, but I push it down, and smile at May. She looks at me, and her eyes soften.

"Sometimes it's better for people to be apart."

"This's true." My parents obviously needed space; it just leaves me picking up the pieces.

"So does your mom work late? Or does she just like to sleep in?" May asks cautiously. This is the hardest part about meeting new people. How do you explain something that's supposed to be simple without telling the whole, big story? I can feel the heat swell up in my cheeks, and I know I'm turning red. I've stayed quiet for too long. May's face contorts.

"You don't have to answer that. I'm sorry. Sometimes I ask too many questions when I'm trying to get to know someone," she says quickly, waving her hands in front of her. I look up at the ceiling and grind my back teeth.

"No, please don't apologize. You're just doing what's normal," I say, rubbing my hands over my face.

"Autumn," May says, taking my hand. "I'm not going to judge you. You don't have to act so mortified." She squeezes my fingers gently and offers me a tender smile. I nod my head and take a deep breath.

"Thank you for being so understanding," I say slowly. "I just—I don't know. My mother's going through a hard time right now. She should be in therapy." I put my hands in my lap and lean sideways out of the blanket.

"My mother goes to therapy." May shrugs her shoulders like it's no big deal. "It's healthy," she says.

"I suppose you're right." Perhaps it is healthy to talk about your feelings, as dreadful a process as that sounds.

May lifts the blanket back over my shoulders and scoots closer to me on the bed. I look out the window and stare through the screen of gray. The rain is still persistent. May's hand rests on my shoulder before trailing down my side. Her fingers circle the small of my back, and the sensation gives me goosebumps. My shoulders become rigid. "Are you alright?" she asks.

"Why wouldn't I be?" I quietly breathe out as I outline the bones lining her neck. Her skin is tanner than mine, like she spends her summers outdoors. Maybe that's why she has so many freckles.

"Trauma doesn't hide well on your face." May smiles in a small sort of way, and I look out the window again. The gray looks like it's changing to white. My head feels light, and my chest is pounding hard, but I know that May's hand offers me a warmth that I've never felt before. I move my fingers away from my side and touch May's arm. Her blue eyes hold mine like a slow rocking cradle as my hand sneaks into hers. Each rock draws me closer, and she guides my head to her shoulder where my cheek rests against her collar bone, and the blanket shields us from the storm. I close my eyes, but am startled by the sound of wood splitting and glass breaking downstairs.

"Autumn!" My mother's voice yells through my closed bedroom door. I can hear her cursing, tearing open filing cabinets. The distant sound of papers flying through the air pulls me away from May, and I jump up.

"I'm up here, Mom, what do you need?" I call back to her. I walk to the stairs and peer down the banister to find my mother rushing from room to room, tearing things apart. "What are you doing?" I yell out, but she doesn't stop. I run downstairs and stand in front of her.

"Where the hell did you put the photo album?" She spits in my face, her arms flaying in front of her, fingers hooked like claws. I stumble back without a word. I peer into the living room. The coffee table is on its side, all the books from the shelf have been thrown across the floor, and the couch cushions are turned up. I look back at the bookshelf and see the corner of the album poking out from behind it.

"I don't know," I tell her. Her eye's narrow, and her lips twitch in anger.

"I know you're lying to me." She pushes me out of her way and goes into the kitchen. She throws everything out of the cabinets and onto the ground. All I can do is watch as she dismantles everything I try so hard to keep orderly. A hand touches my back, and I jump before turning around. I forgot all about May.

"Are you okay?" May peers into the kitchen, but I don't want to scare her.

"Yeah, I'm fine." I try to brush it off as nothing, but my voice cracks. "She's just a little upset right now," I say, shakily.

"Why don't you come to my place while she calms down?" May rubs my arm, and I nod.

"I have to change first." Away from the blankets I'm aware of my damp pajamas, and a chill runs up my spine. May follows me up to my room where I quickly put on a pair of jeans and a t-shirt. My mom's curses become more vivid and creative. I grab my keys and lead May back down the stairs and out the front door. To my relief my mother doesn't follow us outside. I unlock the car doors, and May gets in.

"I'm sorry about all of this." I start the car and back out of the driveway.

"Don't worry." May reaches over and touches my shaking hand. "You have nothing to apologize for." I can't even look at her. I'm so embarrassed that she had to witness all of that. She probably feels uncomfortable. I stop the car in front of the house. Leaving my mother home alone on this rampage isn't a good idea. Without me there to watch her anything could happen.

"Maybe I shouldn't leave." I turn to May but avoid looking at her directly. It feels like I'm covering up for an abusive boyfriend. "I'm just nervous that she'll end up hurting herself." I put the car in park and rest my forehead on the steering wheel.

"Autumn, it's not your responsibility to take care of her, and what can you really do? She's an adult. She'll make her own choices regardless of you." May pushes the hair away from my face, and I know she's right. I just wish my mom made her choices consciously aware that she still has one of her daughters.

"I don't really care anyway," I say.

"Yes, you do." Through the corner of my eyes, I can see May looking at me.

'I just wish I didn't,' I mumble.

I know it's not fair, but I don't think there's any fair way to measure it. My mother's sick, and I don't know how to help her. It's not fair for her either. She should be able to go and see a real doctor, go to a rehabilitation center or something, get some medicine. Did my father leave us with health insurance? I don't know how any of that stuff works, and I doubt my mother does either. She probably doesn't even know that she's ill; how you don't recognize something like that about yourself is beyond me.

The ride to May's is only a few minutes. We run to her front door as quickly as possible.

"You're going to be our first guest." May gives me a small smile and opens the door. We walk into the corridor, and it's almost like walking into a museum. There are dozens of paintings hanging from the walls and lying on the floor.

"Whoa," I say, and smile a little.

"We're still unpacking, so things are a little messy." I step over a luggage set and follow May into the foyer.

"May, do you know where your father put my easel?" A woman wearing a long black robe made of silk walks into the kitchen. She looks just like May but older. Her hair is light brown with one or two small gray streaks. She turns to me and smiles. "Oh, we have a visitor."

"Mom, this is Autumn." May places her hand on my shoulder, and I stare a moment at how put together May's mother looks. Even though her hair's in a messy bun, and she's wearing a nightgown, there's an assertiveness about her movements that leads me to believe she's overcome many trials. Or maybe that's just how I want to see her. I take a step forward and manage to smile.

"Nice to meet you, Mrs.—"

"Please, call me Diana, dear." When she smiles her perfectly white teeth almost seem to sparkle. It'd be extremely unsettling if she wasn't so beautiful. "Are you the one who helped May on her first day of school?" she asks, and I nod my head.

"That was so nice of you. May was so nervous about being new and getting lost. It was trouble enough getting her out of the car. I almost questioned whether or not she was going to skip out and miss it."

"Mom." May steps in and laughs. "You don't have to tell Autumn everything about that morning."

"I know, I know. Would you two like me to fix anything up while I'm in the kitchen?" Diana moves about swiftly, picking up dirty dishes and placing them in the sink.

"No thank you, I'm good," I say. Even though I haven't eaten, I don't have much of an appetite after this morning's events.

"Alright then, I'm going to continue my search in the study. It was very nice meeting you, Autumn. Please stay as long as you like." May's mother leans in close to me as she says the last part. She squeezes my arm and leaves the room.

"My father must be working." May takes out two glasses, fills them with water, and gives me one.

"Thanks." I take a sip from the cup and realize I'm thirstier than I thought. I look out the window above the sink. It's still raining outside. The sky is still dark, and the clouds are still full. I don't want to worry about anything anymore.

"Do you want to go to my room?" May pulls me away from my thoughts, and I oblige. We pass through the hallway again, and I notice that the stairs are completely blocked off.

"Are you renovating the second floor?" I ask May. She pauses next to the steps and looks up at the white blankets that block everything from view.

"The floor boards aren't stable. My father's going to fix it up." She opens up an old wooden door on the opposite end of the house. "I haven't finished unpacking yet, but it's not as messy as the rest of the house." May's room is big and open. There's plenty of walking space even though she has a bed, a dresser, a nightstand, a bookshelf, and a desk. The furniture looks antique, but in good condition. The white flowered wallpaper is peeling in thin patches, but has an eloquent design. The room is cozy, even through the drafts.

"I like it," I say. May walks over to the bed and pulls the blankets flat.

"Have a seat. I'll put some music on for us. What do you listen to?" May lifts a box off the floor and rummages through it.

"Everything," I say. May looks up at me and smiles.

"Alright, well then we'll try this one." She holds up a record and walks over to an old oak turn table. I wonder how many of her possessions are from Europe and how she got them to America. The sound of piano keys serenades the room, and a woman starts to sing in French. "How are you feeling?" I exhale and shrug.

"Fine," I say and cross my arms in front of my chest.

"Get comfortable." May sits next to me on the bed. I can hear the wind thrust into the wood panels along the side of the house, and it reminds me of waves crashing into land.

"You don't have to lie." May crawls further back into the bed and throws me a pillow. She leans her back against the headboard.

"It's sort of a loaded question." I lie down on my stomach and hug the pillow against my chest.

"Do things like that happen often?" she asks. I follow the broken patterns of the wallpaper up to the ceiling and back down again.

"She's going through a hard time right now," I say slowly, even though I already told May this a couple of hours ago.

"How did it start?" May asks softly. "Her hard time?" I think of Mya, and the ache in my heart hums louder. That's a pain I can't escape—the continual hand pressing down against my chest. I feel my lungs writher and breathe in as calmly as I possibly can. I can't talk about Mya yet.

"When I was younger I played this sort of imaginary game." I smile at the memory, and May shifts on the bed so that she's lying next to me. "I'd envision that the woman you met today wasn't my mother. You see, she had the night shift at the hospital, and I hated falling asleep without her, so in my game she'd vanish, and in her place was this other woman. A strong, beautiful lady with a kind-hearted smile. We'd sit underneath a big oak tree, and I'd rest my head on her lap while she ran her fingers through my hair. Sometimes we'd talk, and she'd comfort me, but sometimes we'd just sit in silence. It was nice to have her there with me, to know that she loved me." I look up at May and laugh. "I know it sounds silly to want someone who's not real."

"It doesn't sound silly." May shakes her head, and I look at her.

"It does. I know I sound ridiculous and pathetic. I can't help it though. I just can't be the type of person that people want to hang out with."

"It doesn't really matter to me, Autumn. What other people want," May says quietly. I bite my lip and stop talking. May puts her hand on my back. "I enjoy hanging out with you."

"I shouldn't have said all of that," I whisper, feeling even more embarrassed for the show of emotion.

"It's okay."

"It's just that I've been on my own for so long. I'm not used to having company." I turn to look at May, and her eyes glisten. The music slows down, and May leans in closer to me.

"You don't have to be alone anymore if you don't want to."

"Just like that?" I laugh a little, and heat rises to my face. I know I must be red.

"Yeah."

"That's hard to believe," I say, and May smiles.

"I had a feeling that we'd be friends right when I saw you." May nudges me with her shoulder.

"Really?" I have no idea why she's so interested in me, but I take it as a blessing.

"Why not? You're beautiful, creative, kind."

"You could tell all that just by looking at me?" I laugh at her compliments, but May's expression is serious.

"I could," she says gently, sliding her hand up my back and giving it an encouraging rub.

"I think you're amazing," I say, feeling dizzy.

"Do you?" May asks with her eyebrows arched. I nod,

barely able to concentrate. "You barely even know me, darling." I shake my head back and forth and snap out of it.

"You're the most compassionate person I've met," I say, laying my head on her shoulder. It's the first time I've let someone in since before Mya died. The feeling is so foreign, and my lips tremble at the vulnerability. I close my eyes and rest further into May. She opens her arms, and in one quick motion, holds me. The moment is better than Christmas morning.

CHAPTER 5

I PULL into my driveway and sit in the car for a while. From the outside, everything looks fine. All the windows are intact, there's no yelling, and the door remains on its hinges. It's mid-afternoon, the rain has stopped, and the sky is still dark, but I feel light. I step out of the car and walk slowly to the front of my house. I put my ear to the door and listen. It's quiet.

My body slides down to the cement steps, and I lean against the wood for a few minutes. A kid rides by on his bike, a leaf falls from a tree. The wind carries everything aimlessly. This is my home. I bang the back of my head against the door. If my mom answers then the house will be clean, and everything that happened this morning was just a dream.

I wait and run my hands through my hair. I think of how May's mom squeezed my arm and hugged me when I left. It felt nice. The paint at the bottom of the door is chipping. I stand up and prepare myself to enter into the unknown, but I faintly hear someone call out my name.

"Autumn," Jamie Moore, the boy next door, calls out

from his porch. He stands up, waves his arm, and starts to walk over. Without a doubt, he heard everything that happened. My face is red before he's even in front of me. I try to push out a smile, but there's no point in faking perfection with someone I've known all my life. We were close friends before he gained popularity, a six-pack, and a surplus of girl-friends. That was a long time ago though, and I don't hold any resentment towards him for leaving me behind.

When Mya first got sick, Jamie would come with me to the hospital every other week to see her. When we were younger he'd tell me he was going to propose to her when he turned 18, but that stopped before we even made it to high school, and he definitely never brought it up after her illness.

"Hey Jamie, how's it going?" I look into his candy green eyes, and he scratches the back of his head in a nervous habit, his rusty red hair curling in between his fingers.

"I'm alright, just finishing up some homework." Jamie rolls his eyes and rocks back on his heels. His mother's always been strict when it comes to schoolwork, and I guess it's paid off since Jamie will most likely be our school's vale-dictorian and probably get a scholarship to whichever college he applies to.

"On a Sunday night? That's pretty last minute for you." I poke fun at him, thinking back to the memories of our Saturday morning kickball games, Jamie getting pulled away before noon to read and write.

"Well I guess the old lady has relaxed a bit since I've made it this far. Can you believe we're about to graduate?" Jamie gives me a sad sort of smile. I don't want him to get sentimental now, not after the long day and when it's been at least a month since we've last spoken. His mother prob-ably told him to come over to make sure I was okay. When my parents stayed up late yelling, she'd have Jamie call to ask if I wanted to stay over. It was nice of her, but I could never knock the feeling that Mrs. Moore didn't approve of me.

"The time sure has gone by quickly. How is your mom anyway?" I was a bad influence on Jamie growing up, since I usually got him to sneak outside and skip out on his home-work. We even snuck out at night a few times to go to the park and catch fireflies. She'd always find out and make us stand in her kitchen as she lectured us for at least 20 minutes, but I don't think she ever actually told my parents. If she did, they must've figured she punished me enough.

"Mom is her usual self. My dad's taking her someplace tropical in a few months to ease the pain of me leaving the house." I imagine Mrs. Moore—just below Jamie's shoulders in height—clinging to him in a college dorm room, her husband having to pry her fingers off of him. So sad to leave her baby boy, but so proud of all his accomplishments. I can't help but feel a twinge of disgust at the image.

"That's nice of him," I say quietly, and Jamie digs his hands deep into his pockets while looking over at his house. "It was nice of you to come and say hi." I try to end the conversation before it gets uncomfortable. Besides, it's not like I can ask him inside or even open the door while he's standing in front of me.

"Autumn, if you ever need anything—" Jamie begins, but I cut him off before he can finish.

"You're right next door. Thanks, Jamie." I smile at him, and he smiles back.

"Have a good night, Autumn." Jamie quickly throws his long arms around me and pulls me against his chest. I'm thrown off by the embrace but manage to tentatively squeeze him back before he pulls away. He nods his head, and I watch him walk back to his porch. Jamie was the brother I'd always wanted, and now he's almost a stranger. The distance between our two houses couldn't be greater.

I turn around and rotate the handle, quickly opening the front door. I half expect a naked lunatic to jump out and strangle me, but instead I'm greeted with a messy hallway floor.

"Hello?" I call out and walk into my house. The lights are off in all the rooms, even my mother's. I creak open the door, but it's empty. "Is anybody home?" I call out again. I run up the stairs, hoping to find her in the bathroom. Empty. Everything's empty. What if she went out and got lost? Should I call the police? Do I just leave her? I walk down the hallway to go to my room, but stop in front of Mya's closed door. I stand there without breathing for a minute, then put my hand on the doorknob, and turn. My legs feel weak, but I'm able to step halfway into the room and see that my mother is asleep in Mya's bed. The lamp on the nightstand is on, throwing shadows against the wall. I walk into the room and over to the nightstand. My mom's holding onto Mya's old sock monkey for dear life. I want to rip it out of her arms but decide that it's best not to wake her.

I turn off the light and leave. I go down into the kitchen and start to pick up the broken glass on the counter and the floor. It pricks my skin, and I press on the open cut with my tongue. The bitter taste of my own blood, startling.

I walk into the living room and pull the photo album out from behind the bookshelf. The couch is dismantled, and I search for the cushions so that I can sit down. The room is so messy that the shady blue carpet is completely buried. I try not to think about how long it'll take to clean all of this up. I turn on the lamp and look down at the album. The cover is decorated with faded pink fabric and torn ribbons. It was made when Mya was first born. Her name is on the top and a few years later mine was added on the bottom. The first half of the book includes pictures of only Mya, and the second half has photos of both of us. I open the album to the last couple of pages—when she was 13, and I was 11. We stopped taking pictures when we got older. Mya didn't want there to be any photos of her without hair anyway.

The last photograph in the album is of the two of us sitting on a white and red picnic blanket on the beach. It was late August, but the weather was pretty chilly. That's why we're not in our bathing suits. Mya and I lie on our stomachs facing each other, our heads bent over a notebook. I don't remember what we were doing, probably playing some game that Mya made up. She always created some kind of jigsaw or maze when we were younger. Dad said that she was going to make boards games when she grew up, but Mya always laughed and said that she wanted to do something more interesting. She was a secret space nerd and dreamed of working for NASA. She excelled in all her science classes.

Mya was the real ambitious type. When she wanted something, she went for it. She even graduated high school with her class during her last remission, and that's after she made up all of her missed work while still in the hospital. She didn't want to walk during graduation though, and my parents had to bribe her by taking away her curfew. It's funny how during high school she had to be home before 10, but I could be out all night snorting coke if I wanted, and no one would even notice. Mya would be jealous.

I shut the photo album and stand up. I might as well go lie in bed and try to rest up for another day. I walk to the steps and plan to bring the album to my room to hide, but that leaves more of a chance for my mother to go through my things. I put it back behind the bookshelf. I squat down and notice a picture underneath the chipped wood. It must've fallen out of the album. I lift it towards the light and recognize the image immediately. One of the nurses took it at the hospital right after the transplant. Mya in bed smiling up at the camera with an empty bag of my mother's bone marrow lying next to her. Our mom was the only one who matched Mya's blood enough to give her the marrow. The three of them spent the summer at a nice hospital in Boston about a year ago to get the procedure done. I stayed home by myself most of the time, but I was able to visit for two weeks after the transplant.

It was awful. Mya's skin was cracked, and she was having bad reactions to some of the medication. Every night she'd throw up body tissue because there was nothing left inside of her but herself. My dad lost a lot of weight. I guess with all the stress he was barely able to take care of himself. I'd never seen him so skinny. It took my mom a couple of weeks to walk after they stuck a needle in her back to scrape away the marrow, so I learned how to get around and brought them food every day. I couldn't bring it inside Mya's hospital room because even smelling it would make her nauseous.

I was unsettled, seeing her so helpless. With her bald head, transparent skin, and finger nails peeling away, she resembled a bird that'd just been born. I could barely stand looking at her. I never knew what to say, and I don't think she did either because I can't remember one word exchanged between the two of us during that time. It kills me. She was too busy puking to talk, but I'm sure she would've liked it if I could've thought of something to say. There was just nothing else that mattered at the time.

I bring the photo upstairs with me and shove it underneath my mattress. I don't think my mother should ever see it again, and I don't like looking at it either, but for some reason I can't throw it out. I sit down on the bed, but my body starts to shake. I stand back up and pace through my room, picking things up and putting them back down. I hear my mom open Mya's door and step out into the hallway. I think of the mess downstairs, and my face burns with anger. It's not fair. My stomach turns, and I can't take the shaking anymore. I run into the bathroom, lift open the toilet seat, and throw up until my body feels empty.

"Have you been drinking?" I look up and see my mother standing in the doorway, gazing down at me. I stand up, flush the toilet, and wash my hands. She comes up behind me and looks at me through the mirror above the sink. I look back at her and want to laugh. We both have dark circles underneath our eyes, our lips are chapped, and our skin is clammy.

"I'm going to take a shower. Get out." She doesn't say anything, just slowly turns her head away from me and closes the door behind her. I almost want her to stay, to demand to smell my breath, to actually care if I'd been consuming alcohol. I mean for God's sake, I drove myself home. I put the water on nice and hot and try to relax. I think of May and her big blue eyes. The way it felt when her hands touched me and the way her breath danced against my cheek. The recollection causes a wave of warmth to wash over me, and I make the water colder. I don't even know this girl. Who is she? Why does she want to reside in my life? It can't possibly be because she likes the way I look. I'm average, if that, and she's well-traveled, cultured, experienced. All of the things that I want to be but can't. It just doesn't make sense to me, but there's a lot of things that don't make sense, and I can't be hurt more than I already am.

I turn the water off and wrap a towel tightly around my shivering body. My skin rises in little bumps down my arms and legs, like morning dew covering shards of grass. In my room, I rub away the wetness and put on sweatpants and a tank top. I don't have any homework due tomorrow since this week we're focusing mainly on college resumes. That's not something I have to worry about, so I lend my mind to cleaning up the mess around the house. If anything, I'll graduate high school and become a maid.

I start in the living room with a garbage bag since most of the stuff on the floor is broken or useless anyway. It takes about an hour to straighten up and vacuum, but I know it'll take twice as long to clean the kitchen. I'm not tired though, and I don't think I'll be able to sleep tonight anyway. Not with the weird mixture of feelings between May and my mother. I'm cross between pure rage, excitement, and infatuation. I've never had a friend like May before, and I like it. I like her.

Dissecting my feelings for my mother is more complicated though. Maybe it's just the way I love, but I have a hard time feeling justified in hating her. It'd be normal—I know this—and in some ways, I do hate her. I can't help but see my mother as a little girl though, lost and afraid, raised by a father who showed her no love and a mother who was too young to care about her. In the pictures I've seen of my mother as a child, her and Mya look so much alike. Sometimes their pain whirls into one. Like I said, my mother donated platelets during Mya's transplant. I heard she cried a lot after it happened, and I can't help but feel guilty for resenting her with these thoughts in my mind. I want to love her so badly.

I clean until the sky lightens, and the birds wake with soft chirping. I take a break to sit outside and watch the sun slowly rise above the skyline. It's a beautiful fall morning. I feel like I'm at the circus as I watch squirrels jump from telephone poles and swiftly cross over thin wires. Nature's own acrobatic routine. The new day makes the air clean, and I breathe in as much of it as I can before my stomach starts to grumble. I forgot that I didn't really eat yesterday, and my abdomen is now furious with me. I go inside to the kitchen and scramble myself an egg. I hear my mother slowly open her bedroom door.

"Autumn?" she calls out quietly, but I don't respond. She drags herself into the kitchen and watches me cook. "Autumn, about yesterday, I—" she begins, but I don't want to hear her excuses this early in the morning.

"Do you want an egg?" I cut her off, and she's left with her mouth hanging open. She nods her head, and I add more butter to the frying pan. I can feel her staring at me from the table, but I force myself to stay focused on the slowly cooking yellow of the yolk.

"Where did you go yesterday?" Her voice tries to hold the weight of authority, but with her body slumped forward in the chair and me cooking her breakfast, it all seems pretty sad.

"I went to a friend's house." I wait for her to ask more, but the questions stop there. I put the food on the table and sit down across from her. I have about 20 minutes left before I have to leave for school, so I eat slowly and enjoy each bite. I have work today until 10, so I know it'll be a long day.

"You went grocery shopping yesterday?" My mother's voice cuts through my thoughts, and I look up at her.

"I went on Friday." I watch as she looks back down at her plate and nods her head slowly. I think she actually might want to have a conversation.

"I'll pack you a lunch," she says, and lifts herself up from the table.

"You don't have to." I stand up in front of her, making it impossible for her to get to the fridge.

"I want to," she says quietly. "I want to do this for you."

She looks up at me, and for the first time in my life I realize that I'm a few inches taller than her. I almost can't believe it.

"This is what you want to do for me?" I hesitate and grab her forearm. "Mom..." I feel the anger growing inside my chest, and I squeeze her arm tightly. "This is what you want to do for me?"

She nods her head and says nothing. I'm so conflicted between wanting to thrash her and wanting her to hold me, to give me more than just a sandwich, but instead I sit back down at the table and rest my head in my arms. I stay like this until she puts a brown bag in front of me and then walks back to her room.

When I get to school I immediately go to my locker, switch out my books, and put away my lunch. I try to look for May but don't find her until the bell rings outside of Mr. Busman's classroom. We walk in together and sit in the same two seats in the back. I try to take notes but end up doodling all over my paper. I look over at May. She seems to be paying attention, so I don't bother her. The exhaustion of last night's cleaning session makes it increasingly difficult to keep focus, and I jump in relief when the bell rings.

"I'll see you at lunch?" May asks, and I nod my head while yawning.

"Sorry," I smile sheepishly at her.

"You had a busy night?" May pulls her backpack over her shoulder, and we start to walk out of the room.

"I had a few messes to clean up," I say, looking sideways at her. "And I had a lot on my mind." I immediately think of being held in May's arms, and heat rushes up my neck.

"I hope that's not a bad thing," May says and smiles at me. It's more than enough to hitch my breath. She walks down the hallway, leaving me more dazed then a sleepless night ever could.

I check out during my other classes and keep myself awake by literally counting the tiles on the ceiling until the numbers turn into daydreams, and I'm left with my head in the clouds. Ever since Mya's passing, teachers don't really bother me about my classroom participation. I think the good grades are enough which is more than most students can offer. Besides, what do you say to a student who's been through my trials? I remember when Mya was still alive, how every single day before I walked into a classroom a teacher would ask, "how's your sister doing?" and I'd merely reply "good" because it was impossible to explain that she was actually fading away into nothing, falling even closer to death. Not in that little amount of time before class started. I always figured that if someone really wanted to know how Mya was doing they'd pull me aside, look me in the eyes, and ask with a hand on my shoulder.

Before lunch I run into May while walking up the stairs.

"Glad to see that you're eating today," she says, noting my brown bag. I lift it up awkwardly.

"Yeah, me too." We sit in our regular seats and talk the whole time. I can't help but enjoy her company. It's been awhile since someone's made me laugh during a school day, and May is full of witty comments and funny stories. The lunch my mother made me is even good—a turkey and cheese sandwich with mayo and lettuce, along with a granola bar. Life feels eerily normal, until Casey, an old friend, moves further down the table and stares at me. I look back at her and notice all of my old friends are staring at me too.

"Autumn, are you okay?" Casey asks. Her words are quiet and slow, and it's almost like she's telling me a secret. I nod my head, not liking the sudden attention they're giving me. I don't know why Casey's trying to talk to me now, unless Jamie said something to her, but he knows that I don't really converse with any of my old friends or anyone for that matter.

"I'm fine." I smile awkwardly at them, but they don't look away. I feel my face heat up and know I'm turning red. "Why are you asking me this?" I ask Casey quietly. She looks like she's about to say something but then closes her mouth and looks eagerly at her boyfriend, Ben. He stands up and walks to the end of the table where we sit.

"You're alright, Autumn?" He nods his head, encouraging me to repeat my answer.

"Yeah, I'm fine," I say again, and he stands back up, holding Casey's hand. She remains looking at me though, and I can tell there's something else she wants to say.

"Just making sure," Ben says, and they sit down at the other end of the lunch table. May looks at me and grabs my hand.

"Why don't we spend our lunches in the library? It's hard to hear in here, and it'd be nice to waste a period surrounded by books." May smiles warmly, and I shrug. My old friends haven't spoken to me since the school year began. What sparked their interest now?

"That'd be nice," I tell her, and the bell rings. We walk to English in silence. By the time we reach the classroom, the only empty seats left are apart from one another, so we have to sit separately. Ms. Rogan starts the class by giving a power point on how to make a college resume. She hands us an outline to fill in. We have to type out an official hard copy tonight and hand it in tomorrow. That way she can edit our mistakes, and we can start mailing them in with our applications. Someone in the back of the room raises their hand and Ms. Rogan points a long, slender finger over our heads.

"What if we're not applying to college?" I turn around

and recognize the speaker as one of the boys joining the army upon graduation. It's a valid question though since I don't plan on applying for college either.

"If you're absolutely positive that you're not going to college next year then you don't have to do the assignment, but you still have to stay in class and read our assigned book." I put the resume to the corner of my desk and take out *Beowulf.* I might as well catch up, so I can ace the next quiz. Ms. Rogan sits down at her desk and looks at the sea of students to make sure that we're all working. When she spots me reading I can tell that she's surprised. She stands up from her desk. Shit. I knew she was going to make a big deal about this.

"Autumn." She bends down next to my desk. "Why aren't you filling out the resume?" She touches the paper on my desk and pushes it in front of me.

"I'm not going to college next year," I whisper, looking around the classroom to see a few eyes on us. She notices my discomfort and pulls me out into the hallway. Away from my peers I'm able to breathe comfortably.

"Why don't you want to go to college, Autumn?" Ms. Rogan is at least half a foot taller than me, giving her an even greater essence of authority. I avoid making eye contact and lean against the wall.

"I just don't want to go." I know my response sounds lame. If given the opportunity, maybe I'd like to experience higher education. It just never seemed like a possibility after my dad left, and my mom fell into her depression.

"You're a good student. You can apply for scholarships. Autumn, there are *so* many options out there for you." Ms. Rogan emphasizes that I shouldn't let financial instability hold me back, but that's only one factor of my many concerns of leaving. Who would watch out for my mother? She's in no condition to be left alone. I stay silent, and Ms. Rogan looks down at me with her thin arms crossed and her glasses pushed all the way up against the brim of her nose. I don't like that I'm disappointing her, but my future's not in my own hands right now.

"I appreciate your concern." I look up at her, and she waits for me to say more. "I don't even know what I'd study," I say, and it's true. Even if I did go to college there's nothing that I'm particularly passionate about, nothing that I'd want to lend my entire life to at least. Not in the way Mya wanted to become a scientist.

"Most people don't know what they want to be during their first semester. You'll figure all that out." Ms. Rogan smiles, and even though I know that she's only trying to do what's best for me I really wish she'd let it be. "At least think about it. Maybe you should set up a meeting with Mrs. Nelson. I don't want my best student to go undetected." Mrs. Nelson is our school guidance counselor, and the mere mention of her name makes my skin turn cold. When Mya first got sick she wanted me to set up appointments with her, so she could assess how I was handling the stress. I only met with her once. The memory of sitting in front of her desk and listening to her high-pitched voice bark about death and grief still makes my stomach sink. I was quiet the entire time, and, after noting that my grades were good, she ultimately determined I was fine.

"I'll fill out the resume," I mumble and turn to walk back inside the classroom.

"Autumn." Ms. Rogan puts her hand lightly on my arm. "I don't want to pressure you into doing something you don't want to do. You don't have to fill out the resume, but I do want you to understand that there are options for you." Ms. Rogan holds my gaze until I nod my head. The only reason she knows I'm a good student is because I had her two years ago for sophomore English, and she had one of my literary essays published in the high school magazine. It's nice to have her as a teacher again.

We walk into the classroom, which rapidly quiets down now that the teacher is present, and I sit back in my seat. Even though I don't have to fill out the resume I do it anyway. I catch Ms. Rogan watching me and give her a small smile. Maybe one day I'll need it. After class May asks if I want to hang out after school, and I tell her that I have work for the next three days. We make plans to meet up Thursday, and she walks me to my car.

"How are you getting home?" I ask her. She covers her eyes from the sun with her hands, and I notice a cluster of beauty marks trailing her forearm.

"I was just going to walk. It's not that far." It's not, but I'd love to drive May anywhere.

"How about a ride?" I offer, and she grins, hopping in the front seat. I have about an hour until I have to be at Price's, so I take the back roads and roll down the windows, letting the wind blow our hair. May laughs and waves her hands out the window.

"This feels so good!" She reaches over, brushes a strand of hair away from my face, and then grabs the hand that's not on the steering wheel. My fingers start to tingle.

"I dare you to scream out the window," I tell her, and she lifts her eyebrows. I wait for her to question my request, but instead she sticks her head out the door and yells deep from within her lungs. I smile and pull over along a wooded area.

"What's wrong?" she asks through heavy breathing. Her face is flushed from the air, and I can't stop smiling.

"I've just never had this much fun with someone before," I tell her, and she laughs.

"Oh darling, we've only just begun." May wraps her arms around my neck and gives me a loose hug but doesn't pull away completely. I lean into her, our noses grazing one another. I put my hand behind her neck and pull her into me but get caught by the seatbelt. She leans back and smiles while biting her bottom lip. I smile, hoping that my face isn't as red as it feels.

"I'm going to be late for work." I pull back onto the road, and May changes the radio station. We're quiet for the rest of the ride, but May keeps her hand on my arm. Every few minutes she runs her fingers lightly against my skin. The contact gives me goose bumps and shivers run down my spine.

"I can't wait for Thursday," May says when we get to her house.

"Neither can I." She kisses me on both cheeks before walking off, and I'm on fire for the rest of the night. I'm so energetic at work that Greg pulls me aside and asks if I'm on drugs. I scrunch up my face, flabbergasted at his assumption.

"I'm just happy," I tell him, and he shrugs, dismissing the conversation completely.

"It's nice to see you smiling," Kelvin says when we're behind the counter together. "Did you get a boyfriend or something?" He steps closer to me, and I immediately back away. I shake my head, saved when a customer steps forward and grabs Kelvin's attention. I go in the back to see what boxes I can stock on the shelves. I guess it doesn't really matter to me that May is a girl, but something inside me doesn't want to tell Kelvin, or anyone for that matter, about her. I want May to be my secret, something I can hold onto that'll keep me from sinking. I think she can be that.

CHAPTER 6

THE WEEK DRAGS ON SLOWLY. Between work, school, and sleepless nights, Thursday is like an anticipated gift when it finally rolls around. I'm even awake enough to participate in our Economics class and give a few examples of proper business strategies. May winks at me every time I reply, and before we walk out the door she slips me a piece of folded paper that holds her beautiful penmanship; *I love that you're so smart.* I smile and think maybe I should participate in class a little more often.

We spend lunch in the library like we have the past few days, and it's actually really nice. We sit on a couch in the corner of the room behind all the bookshelves, and the librarian doesn't mind that we eat as long as we keep the space clean of any crumbs. May sits close to me and watches me sketch. She likes to pick something out in the room that I then have to replicate on paper.

"How about the globe?" she asks, pointing towards the sphere of our planet. The globe itself won't be hard, but the window behind it, and the plant hanging from the ceiling will be tedious. I set to work immediately, and May plays with my hair.

"So what do you want to do tonight?" I ask because we haven't really made plans yet, and there's someplace I want to show her.

"I want to take you out to dinner," she whispers in my ear. I turn away from my drawing and look up at her. I've never been on a date before, and I can't help but smile at the thought.

"Where do you want to take me?" I lift my eyebrows, and May rubs her thumb along my jawline in a way that makes me believe she wants to kiss me.

"There's this Italian restaurant in the town next to us that my parents went to last night. They said the food was spec-tacular." I know the exact place she's talking about. My dad brought me there for my birthday dinner last year when Mya was in remission. I don't remember what the food tasted like.

"That sounds wonderful." I smile.

"I can't wait," May whispers on my lips. I inhale her breath and swallow hard. It'll be nice to go out to eat, and it's even better that May picked a restaurant further away. Some-times it's hard to see people I know. They always want to approach me and ask how my mom is doing. I never know what to tell them.

May goes back to playing with my hair, and I continue drawing until the bell rings. She looks down at my sketchbook, but I quickly close it. I don't like to show her the drawings that aren't finished. She gives me a playful scowl before jumping off the couch and pulling me after her. We walk to English in silence, and I notice how comfortable May's quietness is. Her presence has a dream-like effect on me that I can't seem to shake off even when I try to remove my emotions from the picture.

For the first time in my life literature is agonizing. I speed through *Hamlet,* ignoring the in-class readers in the hope it'll make time go by faster, but it's to no avail. Instead I try to think of something romantic I can write in a note to May before class ends. Hamlet is more tragedy than romance though, and the love story isn't one that'll make your heart float. Why can't we read *Romeo and Juliet?* At least they fought to stay together.

May disappears when the bell rings, and I slowly make my way to Math Finance. After dinner tonight, I want to take May down to the river and show her how beautiful this small town can be. I think she'll really like that since she has such a keen eye for nature. That was something that Mya and I differed on. She didn't see things how I saw them. The first time we walked down to the river she got bored within the first five minutes, but I was captivated. The way the sun reflected on the water as it slowly descended behind the trees was enough to take my breath away.

Mya couldn't find comfort in the river like I could. The last day she spent at home she knocked on my bedroom door in the middle of the night and dragged me down to the water. I thought I was dreaming until she stood by the water's edge and started screaming. Tears ran down her face as she threw fistfuls of rocks into the river. I didn't have words to console her, so all I did was watch. I sat in the dirt, in my pajamas, and watched as the moon shone off of her bald head, her frail little arms wrapped around herself. This was my big sister admitting defeat. I haven't really spent much time down by the river since that night, but I really miss it.

I find May standing by my car after school. Her dark hair flies across her face from the wind, and she waves at me. It's a hot day for early October. Some students are even wearing shorts. May has a denim jacket in her arms and wears black jeans with a white blouse. Her curvy figure fills the clothes nicely, and I shuffle in my worn jeans and old fitted t-shirt. I'll have to change before we go out to eat. May throws her arms around me in an embrace and her hair whirls in my face.

"Do you want a ride?" I open the passenger door for her, but she shakes her head and pushes it closed.

"Not today. I'm going home to get ready, and you're going to pick me up at six." May holds my hands and squeezes them together.

"You got it," I tell her. She gives me a wink and quickly turns around.

When I open the front door to my house my mom is on the couch eating a sandwich. She's been getting up every day and eating on a schedule, which I'm very thankful for, but she still sleeps late and goes to bed before the sun is even down. I have to be friendly and encouraging because I know it'll take time for her to adjust to a normal lifestyle, but I can't help my resentment. It's been so long since I've had a mother who provides any type of support or comfort. Even if she does come around, how can I allow myself to trust her again?

"Hey, Mom." I nod my head and put my backpack down on the empty seat next to her. I watch as the muscles near her mouth twitch, and I think she wants to offer me a smile but can't.

"How was school?" she asks. I pick up the paper plates and napkins littering the coffee table.

"Educational," I answer flatly. I bring the garbage into the kitchen and throw it out. "How was your day?" I call out to her. Somehow the kitchen is filled with clutter. The deli meat and mayonnaise sit out on the kitchen table, spoiling, when they should be in the fridge. I'm glad she's eating, but can't she clean up after herself too?

"I watched TV." My mother's soft voice somehow manages to travel to my ear. I don't answer her though because I know the conversation is over. Besides, what I really want to ask is if she can stop being such a slob, but that will discourage her, and I'd hate myself if she resorted back to starvation. Instead I go upstairs and immediately open my closet. The nicest thing I own is the black dress that I wore to Mya's funeral. I went to the mall by myself and picked it out quickly without even trying it on. Luckily it fit but not well enough. It hung too loose over my shoulders, and I kept having to pull it up over my chest. The funeral was already so uncomfortable though. A girl swimming in a pillowcase didn't draw anyone's attention.

I dig deeper into my closet and pull out a brown box. It holds all the clothes Mya gave me when she first got sick. I've never worn any of them, and I don't know if I can now. Even if I felt comfortable enough, I'm sure it'd upset my mother. I don't have nice clothes to go out in, and I know there's a skirt or two in here that will probably fit me. Mya did give me these clothes in anticipation that one day I'd wear them, whether she was here to see me or not.

I open the box and start to dig through. I've had the clothes for a long time—over three years now—but when I hold up one of her shirts to my face I swear I can still smell Mya. I rub the fabric against my cheek, and the hollowness in my chest aches. Mya was always bigger than me, but after the transplant she barely weighed 90 pounds. She hasn't worn these clothes in a long time. The scent is a ghost or a remembrance of some sort. I put the clothes back in the box and stuff it in my closet. I can't wear them tonight.

My mother's closet is free game though, and I dig through

her blouses and dress pants, looking for something young. She has a pair of tan khaki pants that fit me perfectly and a light blue button up. I try the outfit on and look in the mirror. My hair is a mess, but the outfit will work. I strip naked and take a quick shower. The anticipation of spending the night with May has me so excited that my stomach is a jumble of nerves. It takes me all of 20 minutes to get ready, and I'm left to pace around the kitchen looking for something to do.

"You look like me." My mother's voice surprises me, and I jolt. She stares at me strangely, a thin straight line plastered over her face, as rigid as her body. She seems tense.

"I look nice then?" I ask, turning to her so that she can assess my appearance. Not that she's any type of fashion critic, but I do need someone to tell me that I don't look horrible.

She nods her head slowly. "Where are you going?" She leans one hand on a kitchen chair and places the other one on her hip.

"Out," She doesn't deserve to know my location just because she brushed her teeth this morning. Besides, she'll be in bed long before I get back.

"You could be my sister," my mother whispers, her eyes fixed on me. We do look a lot alike, and in her clothes, I probably appear older. I don't want to be my mother's sister though, so I turn around and focus on wiping down the counter. I can feel her soft brown eyes following me, and when I turn around she's crying.

"Mom," I say in a surprised whisper. "What's wrong?" I put my arms around her and pull her close to me. She sobs against my chest. I can almost feel the misery projecting off of her with each heavy shake.

"I—oh, Autumn!" She gasps for air, over and over again, until she can finally speak. "I hate what my life is," she chokes out and hiccups. I have to be patient because more than anything I detest that I'm holding my mother like a child, but I want to help her. I think. I just hate that this is what it is. The guilt is enough to consume me.

"You know, Mom," I say quietly. "You can change this. You can start going to work again. If you regain some type of structure, it'll make living easier." It's exactly what I had to do. I didn't go to school for two weeks after Mya's funeral. Sitting alone in my room, and facing the stillness, the quietness, was enough to make me want to kill myself.

"It's not that easy." My mom sniffles. "I turn around and expect to see you and your sister sitting at the table doing homework, your father watching some television show, but it's so empty." She backs away from me and cries into her hands. I rub her back and pull out a chair for her to sit.

"This isn't going to be easy." I wait until she's sitting and then pour her a glass of ice cold water. "We all have to move on though." I didn't want to stop mourning either, but I had to. I was too hungry to grieve. Someone had to be responsible and feed our starving stomachs.

"Well, your father did a great job at that," my mother spits out bitterly, like someone dipped her tongue in vinegar. I want to tell her that it's her fault he left, that he couldn't handle her condition, but I know that's wrong.

"Just focus on yourself. You need to get better." I put my hand on her shoulder and feel her whole body sink forward. "Drink the water, Mom." I push the cup closer to her and leave to grab my bag from the living room. I don't want to be late for my first date, but I feel bad for leaving my mother when she's like this. I ease the guilt by kissing her on the forehead, a gesture I haven't made in years, and run my fingers soothingly through her hair.

"Autumn," she says, turning to me. She catches my

fingers and gives them a small squeeze. "Thank you." The words are unexpected, and I feel awkward receiving her gratitude. I nod my head silently and wonder if she can see—through my eyes—my pain, like I can see hers.

I drive to May's house slowly so that I have time to distance myself from what happened in the kitchen, and so I can calm the nerves that vigorously thrash against my stomach's walls. I guess it's good that my mother is communicating her grief with me. Maybe it's a step in the right direction, but I don't want to get my hopes up. When I pull in front of May's house I feel calmer, probably because I'm so excited to see her and I don't want to screw anything up by acting too nervous. I walk up to her front door and knock loudly.

"Autumn." May's mother throws her arms around me, and I lean into her. She holds me in a comforting embrace, but I pull away, not used to the affection. Diana still grasps my arm though, and leads me into the house. "May told me you two are going out to dinner?" she questions, and I nod my head. She brings me to May's room and knocks on the door.

"One minute." I hear May call out. Diana shakes her head and clicks her tongue.

"She's been getting ready for over an hour." I take the length in time to mean that May will look absolutely beautiful —well, even more beautiful than she already is naturally, and that I'm probably very underdressed. "Why don't we wait in the living room? God knows how long a minute will actually last." Diana sits next to me on an old Victorian style couch that sinks too far back against the decorated wooden frame.

"So how do you like living here so far?" I ask, trying to make small talk.

"Oh it's just gorgeous. It's like we've walked right into a

Robert Frost poem." I smile at the reference. I feel like Diana is watching me very closely, and I blush under her gaze. "So Autumn, what colleges are you looking at for next year?" Diana has her legs crossed, and she sits so that we're facing each other. For some reason, I feel ashamed telling May's mother that I'm not applying anywhere.

"I don't know yet." I shrug and act like it's not that big of a deal.

"You have time. I didn't go to college right after high school. Sometimes it's best to figure out what you want first," she says. No one's given me advice like this yet. Usually schools pressure you into continuing education, saying that if you stop you most likely won't go back, that you'll end up stuck with a low wage job your whole life. By the looks of it though, Diana's done well for herself, and she's doing what she likes.

"I really like art," I say quietly, the words slipping through before I can second guess them.

"May told me you have skill." Diana smiles. "Classes are good, but you can get pretty far with lots of practice." She moves her hands when she talks, and it's easy to see where May gets her mannerisms.

"Okay, I'm ready." Our attention immediately turns to May who walks into the living room and stands in front of us. The first thing I notice is her perfume. The scent wafts over me, and I'm dreamily intoxicated while trying to take in the rest of her appearance. May is in heels, so she's a few inches taller than me. She wears a beautiful black dress with a floral lace print near the chest.

"You're beautiful," I say, forgetting that Diana is sitting right next to me. She doesn't seem to care though because she jumps up and throws her arms around her daughter.

"You are so grown up." Diana kisses May on the cheek,

who blushes at the attention while giving me a sheepish smile. Her dark red lipstick matches her outfit perfectly. Diana is right; May looks like an adult.

"Sorry for making you wait so long." May directs the statement at me. Her blue eyes seem darker than usual but still shine like a lighthouse, guiding me to her. I stand up, and May takes my hand.

"It's fine. I had a nice time talking to your mother." Diana nods to me, and I give her a smile. Even though Diana's features are a little bit older, there's no doubt May is her daughter.

"You two have fun and be safe." Diana points her finger at May, who rolls her eyes.

"We're going out to eat not joining a gang," May jokes but gives her mother a kiss before walking out the door. I give Diana a hug, and she tells me to keep her daughter out of trouble. I nod my head assuring her that we'll be careful. I can't help but admire how protective she is. It's obvious that Diana cares a lot about her daughter. I'm glad that May has this kind of support.

I open the door on the passenger's side for May to step in and wait until she's fully seated before I close it. It feels funny to be so formal, but with May looking beautiful beyond my wildest dreams I feel I should treat her like royalty. When I get in the car the first thing May does is giggle in excitement.

"It's going to be a good night," she tells me, holding my hand the entire ride. When we pull into the parking lot it's hard to find a spot. The restaurant looks busy.

"Do you think that they'll have room for us?" I ask.

"I don't mind waiting if you don't." May shrugs carelessly, and I brush a piece of hair back behind her ear.

"You are absolutely stunning." I look into her eyes so she understands how much I mean the statement.

"Thank you, darling." She rubs her thumb lightly along my jaw, and we step out of the car. Even the entrance is pretty full. I didn't think it'd be this crowded on a Thursday night.

"How many?" The hostess asks, looking at me.

"Two," I tell her, and May holds my hand. The woman is probably my age or younger. She chews gum so fresh that when she bends over her notebook I smell mint.

"There's about a 15 minute wait," she says. I look over at May, and she nods her head as if to say it's not too long.

"Okay, we'll wait." I give the hostess my name, and she points to some benches outside, saying that she'll call me when they're ready. Since mostly everyone waits inside it's quiet in the fresh open air, and we sit together comfortably.

"How's your mom doing?" May breaks the silence.

"Good," I say, but it's a force of habit reply, and I know that I don't have to hide from May. "It seems like she might actually be getting better. She, uh, thanked me today," I say slowly.

"What did she thank you for?" May rubs her fingers lightly over my forearm, back and forth, like the willows blowing in the wind. Her touch tickles me gently.

"I'm not exactly sure." I don't know if she thanked me for the comfort I gave her in the moment or if she realized how much I actually do for her. "I feel like if she really appreciated me, she'd offer me more than just those simple words." I look at May and wait for her reaction to my statement. I'm not sure if what I'm feeling is selfish or not: to want more than what my mother has already struggled so much to give. Two weeks ago, when she was a puddle of despair on the couch I would've given anything to hear her say something like that to me, but now it's not enough, and I don't know what is.

"Hopefully in time she'll recognize how lucky she is to have a daughter like you." May squeezes my hand and leans close into me so that her lips graze my ear. "Until then let me appreciate you, and maybe that will help fill your void." May kisses behind my ear, and I moan quietly. I'm just about to turn and kiss her fully when the hostess calls out my name. May winks at me as we stand. I follow her to a table in the back, and she places a menu in front of me.

"Is someone meeting you here?" she asks, eyeing the empty seat. May must've gone to the bathroom.

"Yes, she'll be right back," I tell her, and she puts another menu on the table. I watch her walk away and look around at the full tables, relieved not to see any familiar faces. The smell of basil and fresh baked bread wafts through the air. My father used to say that you could tell a restaurant was good when the aroma made your mouth water. It's no wonder why he liked this place.

"Hey, sorry about that," May says, pulling out her chair. She picks up the menu, and I look down at my own.

"They usually serve family style dishes here. Do you want to get something to share?" I ask. May sets down her menu and rubs her thumbs over the table cloth.

"Spaghetti and meatballs?" she suggests. It doesn't get any more romantic than that.

"Sounds perfect." It's one of my favorite dishes. I set my menu on top of May's and lean into the table. "Your mother's a lovely person," I say, and take a sip of my water.

"She's very kind." May gives me a small smile, and her eyebrows twitch together.

"What's wrong?" I ask, confused by her sudden change. May shakes her head lightly, and her smile widens.

"Nothing's wrong. I was just thinking about how marvelous of a woman she is." May's eyes sparkle lightly in admiration when she says this. "I try not to take her for granted." Under the table I feel May's foot press against me, and my face feels hot.

"I can't get over how beautiful you are," I say, my breath quickly exhausted.

"You better control yourself." May points a threatening finger at me.

"I'll try, but no promises," I tease, grabbing her finger and curling my hand into her fist. May leans forward to place a quick kiss on my fingers.

"I'm glad we're here together." May smiles and looks me in the eyes. I stare into her pupils, and for a moment, I can see my life with her. The two of us cuddled together watching TV, cooking each other dinner, taking evening walks in the snow.

"It's nice to have you." My head feels heavy, and I quickly shake it off.

"You have me?" May lifts an eyebrow and runs a finger along the palm of my hand. "I didn't know I was so committed to you."

"Do you want to be?" I ask, feeling a little nervous, but May smiles, her cheeks emitting a soft glow.

"I'd really like that. Would you?" May looks almost anxious, and if I wasn't blushing already, I definitely am now.

"I enjoy holding your hand every day," I mumble, and May's eyes soften.

"That's very poetic of you." Her words are a whisper, and they echo in my head.

A young man in his early 20's approaches our table. His black hair is gelled back, and there's a glisten of sweat on his upper lip where it looks like he's just shaved. He pulls out a black rectangular notepad and clears his throat.

"My name is Tyler, and I'll be your waiter this evening. Is there anything I can get you to drink?" His eyes dart into mine and then quickly scan the room. He seems nervous, his hands twitching when the pen hits paper. I wonder if this is his first night.

"Water is fine." I look at May, and she nods her head. I give him the rest of our order, and he scribbles it into the black book.

"Anything else for you, miss?" he asks. I shake my head, and he grabs the menus and shuffles to another table.

"So," May says, drawing my attention back to her. "What do you like to do for fun?" The question is simple enough in essence, but I can't even answer it. I let out a sigh, and May's smile fades away into concern.

"May, I have to be honest with you." I let go of her hand and start to wring my fingers together in my lap. "After my sister passed away I lost my friends, what was left of my family, and what little social life I had. It's mostly my fault." I don't want May to think I have any resentment or anger towards my old friends; they tried to help me when everything first happened, but I pushed them away and told them I was fine when I wasn't. "I kept my life hidden because I was afraid of what might happen if people saw what a disaster it was. I don't have fun. I go to work, I go to school, and I take care of my mother."

May nods her head slowly when I finish talking, and I can see her biting the inside of her lip, negotiating what to say.

"I guess I kind of knew that already. I should rephrase my question." May reaches for my hand again, and I give it to her. "What *would* you like to do for fun?" She smiles softly at me, and I give her a crooked smile back.

"There's these mountains a little south from our town. I've always wanted to hike them," I say, shyly.

"Then we'll do it." May kisses my fingertips, and I notice how warm her lips are.

"Do you like the outdoors?" My thumb grazes her bottom lip before I put my hand back on the table.

"My mother's an artist. I've spent most of my life outside." May probably sees things the same way I do. She'll love the river.

"Here you are." Tyler, our waiter, comes up from behind me and sets a steaming plate of spaghetti down on our table. "It's hot. Be careful," he says.

"We will be." I smile, and he gives me an awkward smile.

"This looks great." May picks up her fork and starts to rummage through the noodles. I turn back to the waiter, but he's already gone. We eat through the pasta pretty quickly, and it's really nice sharing a meal with someone. By the time the plate is clean I'm fuller than I've been in a while.

"You look beautiful," May says, setting down her fork. "Especially when you're happy." She folds her hands below her chin and rests her head against them.

"Am I happy right now?" I ask, raising my eyebrows.

"Darling, you're glowing," she says. I laugh loudly, and a few people turn to stare at me.

"Well, this is thanks to you I guess. Here's to as many happy days as we want." I raise my glass in a toast, and she clinks her cup against mine. A few people from nearby tables watch us, and I start to feel uncomfortable.

"Ask for the check when he comes by," May says, noticing the audience as well. I make eye contact with Tyler, and he walks right over.

"All done?" He picks up the empty plate. "Anything for dessert?" He sets a smaller menu on the table, but I shake my head. May puts her hand on top of mine and bends her head down as other guests point at us.

"Can we just get the check?" I ask, anxiety quickly growing inside my chest. Tyler looks between May and me, and I can't tell if his facial expression is one of confusion or disgust. He bites his tongue and sets down a black leather folder.

"Have a good night." He walks away slowly, and I hear him mumble something underneath his breath, but I can't make out what.

"Let's get out of here," May says, and I can tell she feels uncomfortable. I put some cash in the folder and leave it on the table. We walk out of the restaurant quickly and go straight to the car. I don't know what to say, so I turn on the radio, and we listen to music while I drive us back into town. When I pass May's street she asks me where we're going. I grip the steering wheel and push gently on the breaks as we descend a hill.

"I'm taking you to the river," I say.

"I hear it's beautiful," she says, casually waving her hand out the window.

"May, I want to tell you everything." I keep staring in front of me, but I can feel May's gaze on the side of my face. She brushes a few strands of hair behind my ear, and I lightly lean into her hand.

"I'd love that," she says, and this time I scream out the window.

CHAPTER 7

I PARK the car near the boating dock and lead May to the walkway that circles the river. We stop and sit on a metal bench next to a dimly lit street lamp, illuminating us enough so that we're not completely in the dark. The sun has already set. If you look towards the northern end of the river the sky still holds a few shades of violet blue that contradicts the darkness wrapping around the southern end. I love looking back and forth at the two sides, and I point out the display to May.

"It's like we're sitting in between two choices," May whispers.

"I wouldn't know which side to choose if that's the case." I've tried countless times to capture this night sky on paper, but it never comes out the way I want it to.

"Whenever you're ready to talk, darling, I'm listening." May links our arms and leans into me. I take a deep breath and stare out into the water.

"Four years ago my older sister, Mya, was diagnosed with Acute Myeloid Leukemia." It's hard to describe what I want to say. My emotions pound inside of me like a beast wanting to escape. It's probably best to start from the beginning. "We were really close growing up. It wasn't like your usual sisterly bond where two girls fight over a curling iron. Mya was my best friend. We looked out for each other." I think back to the time when Mya showed me how to open a locker before my first day of middle school because she knew I would've spent the whole night worrying about it. In many ways Mya was my safety blanket, especially in social situations. I'd get so anxious before a school dance or a party, and she wouldn't leave my side until I felt comfortable.

"I was so scared when my dad told me what she had. He woke me up at five in the morning after spending the entire night in the emergency room. We thought Mya had pneumonia and that that's why she was so sick. My parents only brought her to the hospital because she was having trouble breathing. They never thought she was dying." I remember that night very clearly because I was mad I had to stay home. I'd spent most of the night waiting up for them and leaving messages on their voicemail. I don't even know how I fell asleep. I look at May who quietly watches me. She offers a small smile and squeezes my arm.

"Go on," she whispers in my ear.

"I didn't really know what Leukemia was. I just knew that it was a kind of cancer, but people survive cancer all the time." I feel my throat tighten up but push past it. "When I asked my dad if Mya was going to die he couldn't give me an answer. I was confused because Mya was so young, and it didn't make sense that her life was being threatened. All of that happened—I found out about the cancer, realized she might not survive—and then immediately went to school. How crazy is that? My dad was going back to the hospital and I couldn't see Mya until that afternoon anyway because of tests. Supposedly, it was a better way to pass the time.

"Mya's friends asked me if she was okay when she didn't show up to homeroom. I guess they knew she went to the hospital the night before. I told them she had cancer, and they were distressed. So distressed they even cried, something I had yet to do." I think back to the group of girls who used to sleep over my house on Friday nights. I used sneak into the hallway and listen outside of Mya's room so that I could hear what they talked about. A lot of boy drama and even one pregnancy scare. They're all in college now, but if they ever see me in town they make sure to hug me and ask how I'm doing.

"You didn't cry when you found out?" May asks, and I shake my head.

"I was so numb. It's like my body shut down those first few weeks. I didn't cry about it until a year later, when the chemo didn't work, and we realized we'd have to do it all over again. After that I think I cried a lot because it was even less likely she'd live." I remember overhearing the news when my mom was on the phone with a doctor. She was crying, and I could hear her from outside. I knew to enter the house quietly. When she hung up she saw me standing by the front door. She told me matter-of-factly, like there was no other way to say it, and I liked hearing it that way because there really was no other way to say it. We were already so tired and emotionally drained. Why make the truth even more dramatic than it had to be?

"Are you alright?" May asks, planting a kiss softly against my cheek. I nod my head, still looking straight ahead.

"It was difficult seeing Mya that way for so long. It was like being in a car crash for years."

"That sounds traumatizing." May squeezes my hand again, and I move closer into her.

"Every day I'd wake up, not knowing if she was dead,

and some days I'd want her to be. She was in so much pain it made me sick." I think back to the allergic reactions she had to the medications. One time her whole body was covered in a rash that burned her skin. She couldn't move or wear clothes or even breathe without feeling excruciating pain. I look over at May and stare into her eyes. "It was horrible," I whisper and swallow hard.

"That all must've been a lot for your family to go through."

"Yeah well, we kind of fell apart. The only reason my parents stayed together the whole time was because they didn't want to put Mya and I through even more shit. I mean, not getting divorced didn't help the situation much either. They hated each other. When Mya was home from the hospital they tried putting on a show so she'd feel more at ease, but I noticed everything. Sometimes they'd come close to throwing blows." I shake my head, thinking of the afternoon exchanges where they'd switch night duty. The stress and exhaustion of weeks spent in the hospital made them snap at each other in hysteria.

"You probably went undetected during this time, huh?" May asks, and a bitter chuckle escapes my mouth.

"I could rebel all I wanted to if that's what you mean." Besides smoking pot a few times with Mya and her friends, I didn't really do anything illegal. I was too busy trying to keep the house clean for Mya's weak immune system.

"It's not." May's lips twitch slightly. "I meant that no one was there to protect you." Her words make my stomach sink, and I feel my face turn pale.

"I didn't need anyone. Mya needed my parents help. She was dying," I say, and May frowns at me.

"That doesn't mean that you didn't need them as well." It feels like May can read my mind, and I don't think I like it.

Not when I've worked so hard to block everyone out. But this is what I wanted. I want to tell May everything. It feels like too much though. The amount of trauma isn't relatable. If I wrote my life as a story I'd be criticized for my protagonist suffering excessively, and it'd be too much for a reader to handle. I don't want to overwhelm her.

May squeezes my hand.

"Autumn, I promise that you don't have to hide from me." I breathe in and look down.

"I did need them." My voice is tiny, and I cough a few times, trying to clear the anxiety leaking from my throat. "I just felt like I was old enough to take care of myself, and they were always so busy. They didn't have time for me." I let go of May's hand and rub my face fiercely. Dammit.

There, I destroyed my man-made fence, letting everything out, letting everything in. I wrap my arms around my stomach and rock forward, letting out a low moan. May puts her hand on my back and rubs it gently. I take slow, deep breaths. I don't want this to turn into an anxiety attack.

"Autumn, take your time. It's okay." May runs her fingers through my hair and pulls it out of my face. I nod my head and sit up straighter.

We sit quietly for a while, watching the tide carry the water back and forth. I even see a few fish jump into the night air. It's nice to be back by the river.

"I'm glad that I found you," May says, and I realize she's been watching me.

"Why is that?" I give her a small smile and look down at the ground.

"Because, you don't have to be alone anymore." She closes my hand around her own, and I stand abruptly, pulling her forward.

"I want to show you my favorite spot," I say and lead her

down the walkway to where the willows grow. We crawl in front of them and lie down on the grass. May looks beautiful in the moonlight. Her dress is pulled up around her thighs, revealing tan, muscular legs. I imagine them intertwined with my own but shake the thought from my mind. It's been awhile since my skin has seen the sun.

"This is breathtaking," May says, waving both of her arms up towards the sky. The stars go on for miles, and it's rather amazing. "I don't think heaven could match this type of scenery." She smiles at me, and I'm beyond delighted that she enjoys the river this much.

"I don't believe in heaven anyway," I say after a moment. "Or hell."

"Why not?" May turns on her side and looks at me.

"It's just something that people made up to comfort themselves with the thought of dying," I tell her. "The bible or whatever doesn't even make sense."

"The thought of burning in hell for eternity isn't very comforting, and most religions don't make sense." May smiles.

"That's how they end up controlling you. You end up doing everything out of fear. And God," I breathe out a bitter laugh. "Love me or die forever, an afterlife of eternal suffering. How messed up is that? That kind of forced love isn't real." I shake my head. Mya hated it when groups from churches would come in gatherings and fill her hospital room. They'd pray over her for hours. It was my dad's idea. He was religious in that way, but the rest of us weren't. It's hard to believe in God when someone you care about is dying, but my mother told us that it's his way of dealing with the situation and asked us not to complain.

"I guess I don't really believe in heaven either," May says, laying her head against the ground.

"I hope that when you die you get another chance," I say while looking for the Little Dipper in the sky.

"What do you mean?"

"Like you relive your same life, but know everything that happened in your previous one, so you can change whatever you did wrong or didn't like." It's not perfect, but maybe if I knew that Mya would get cancer I could've told my parents to take her to the hospital earlier. Maybe there would've been more of a possibility of her survival. Or I could've at least comforted her better.

"A life full of second chances," May says, and I can hear the smile in her voice.

"A new beginning," I tell her.

"That all sounds nice, but in your new beginning we may never meet." She stretches her arms back towards the sky, and I grab one of her hands.

"I'd just have to find you. I'd still have all of my old memories, so it wouldn't be that hard." I wiggle my fingers in between hers and rub my thumb against the bones in the back of her hand like a xylophone.

"But what if after you've changed everything in your life you didn't want to meet me? You might be perfectly content living with Mya and your white-picket-fence family."

"No," I say quickly, pausing for a moment to collect my thoughts. "I'd always remember what this feels like, lying next to you in the grass. I'd feel a strong absence that couldn't be settled until I found you again."

She turns over on her side and slides her fingers through my hair. Her lips lightly touch mine in a soft kiss. When she pulls away I can't breathe. My chest is on fire from her zeal and my spill of emotions. I put my hand on top of my heart and inhale deeply. She laughs while biting down on her lower lip.

"I wouldn't want to live again without you. I don't even think I could." She puts her arms around me and blows the words into my ear. Everything she does feels so good—a welcomed bliss to my reality.

"Who are you?" I ask dreamily. I close my eyes and breathe in the scent of May's perfume lingering on her neck.

"I'm a girl living in a small town, who's fallen in love with another girl who lives in a small town," May says, slowly.

"That sounds like who you are right now, but that can't be who you've always been," I say, my lips itching for a second kiss.

"I was nobody, love. I didn't exist before I met you," May says, smiling. She pushes her head down and kisses me hard on the lips. "This is who I am." Her hands roam up my sides, and she holds me tightly against her. I've never felt safer in my whole life.

"Don't leave me tonight," I whisper in her ear. May stares into my eyes, and her lips twitch downward.

"I can tell that you're exhausted. You need to get some sleep, and if I'm there I know that'll be hard for you to do." May's voice is filled with concern, and I can't blame her for worrying. It *has* been awhile since I've slept more than a few hours at a time. She stands up and offers me her hand. We walk back to the car with our arms linked, and I silently say goodbye to the river. Now that I've been down here with May it feels like it'll be easier to come back and visit. I drive May to her house and walk her to the front door where she leans forward and kisses me.

"Get home safe," she tells me. I nod my head, feeling the weight of exhaustion she must've seen in my eyes. I arrive home quickly and check around the house to make sure everything is in order. My mom's in her room with the television on, and when I open the door she calls out Mya's name sleepily. I walk out, letting her believe the dream.

When I get to my room it takes everything from me to strip out of my clothes and put on a pajama shirt. I turn off the lights, and as soon as my head hits the pillow my eyelids are too heavy to keep up. I think of May, how her arms felt around me. I imagine that she's still holding me and can almost feel the heat of her breath on the back of my neck when I drift away.

CHAPTER 8

WHEN I ARRIVE at work I hear Greg in the back office yelling. I give Kelvin a questioning look, but he just shrugs. I peak my head in and see Greg hunched forward in his desk with the phone pressed tightly to his ear so that his skin has turned red. A few beads of sweat drip down the back of his neck which would probably tickle if he wasn't so entranced in conversation. I leave poor Greg alone and see what Kelvin has done so far.

"Has it been busy?" I ask him, and he shrugs again.

"Not really. There was a rush at lunch, but that's about it."

"Do you want to man the counter while I clean off the shelves?" During my last shift I noticed that dust had built up on various sections of the store.

"Sounds good," Kelvin says, throwing me a rag. I smile at him, about to turn around when I notice his lips pulled heavily downward, his eyebrows shoved tightly together.

"Kelvin, what's wrong?" I ask, softly. He takes a deep breath and hits the toe of his shoe against the tile floor.

"I know it's not much, but I kind of like this job." I wait for him to explain more. He opens his mouth a couple of times and taps his shoe faster. "I don't want to work at the Super Center. I like interacting with people on a personal level, here, in our home town. I know that a five minute conversation while ringing up a customer isn't much, but it's my favorite part of the day," Kelvin says and stops taping his foot.

"Did Greg fire you?" I whisper, confused as to why he'd have to leave Price's.

"No, Autumn, but isn't it obvious? Price's isn't going to last much longer. We'll both be out of work." Kelvin has a point. I don't want to work at the Super Center either, but I will if I have to. Kelvin could also get a job there even if he didn't like it. It's better than not having anything. Besides he'd probably do well in customer service. As long as a glass or counter is between him and the customer.

"You'll find something after this. I bet Greg would give you a killer recommendation." I think of their little porn trade and offer Kelvin a small smile.

"I guess."

Greg comes out of the back office, and Kelvin and I turn away from each other.

"I'm getting some air," Greg says and walks out of the front door. What is he going to do if he loses the store? I wonder if his dad has another company he could join. Perhaps Mr. Price wouldn't trust him though after this one goes down. But it really isn't Greg's fault. This town is full of lower-middle class people who'd rather get a better deal than support a small, local business. They probably don't even realize that shopping at the Super Center hurts Greg's store.

I walk to the back of the store and start dusting off soup cans. When Mya was sick the whole town rallied to fundraise for us. The elementary and middle school did penny drives, churches threw dinners—which the local grocery store donated food to—the high school sports teams held car washes. All sorts of groups chipped in. It was such a big help during the time.

I'm too deep in thought to notice Jamie watching me a few feet away. He's in a tank top and gym shorts with a blue sports drink held loosely in his hand.

"Hey, Autumn." He smiles and walks closer. "How's it going?"

"You know, same shit different day," I say and smile back. "Were you running?" I ask, noticing his damp hair.

"I just finished football practice. Your boss is standing outside power smoking cigarettes." He runs his hand through his hair, making it more disheveled.

"He's not having a good day." I glance through the big front windows and see Greg pacing back and forth. "How's football going? Are you guys winning this season?"

"Not bad, we're playing a lot better than last year." Jamie pats the top of his head and tries to tame his hair. "The school is cutting a lot of our funding though. Morale is down." It looks like everyone's having money troubles.

"I'm sure the homecoming game will cheer everyone up," I say, trying to be positive.

"Hopefully. You should come."

"Maybe." I don't like going to school events, but I feel bad not watching Jamie play.

"It's a few weeks away, so you have time to think about it." Jamie gives me a wink and waves as he turns away. "Have a good night, Autumn."

"You too," I call after him and watch as he checks out and leaves the store. I'm not a creep or anything, but watching Jamie is like watching what my life could've been like if Mya didn't get sick. I'd be a normal teenager, going to football games and dances, and Jamie would still be my close friend.

I watch as he chugs his drink and throws it in a garbage can on the side of the street. He brushes the sweat away from his brow with his shirt and jogs off slowly. It was hard for him once Mya died. He cried once to me, when he found out it happened. We didn't talk at all because it was so soon, the pain too raw. I think it was easier for me because I'd seen the slow progression of her body deteriorating. In the end, I knew it was coming. It was just hard to stomach. Jamie didn't come by after it got too bad, partly for his own good. I don't think Mya wanted him to see her like that. When he found out his mouth hung open, and his long limbs clung to my body, trying to stay stable. I knew then that it wouldn't be the same between us. He was mourning, and I felt nothing. My dead sister getting buried, just another day.

Greg walks back into the store, and the smell of cigarettes is overwhelming. He goes into the back room, and Kelvin and I exchange glances. I wish there was something we could do to help him. It just seems like this town can't sustain itself. Not with how run down it is. Almost every house needs a new paint job. The roads are bumpy and ridden with potholes. Even with the disrepair it has a certain charm though. There's beauty here, especially with the river.

At the end of my shift I don't want to leave because Greg hasn't moved from his back office. It's hot, and I can smell his sweat. I give the door a soft knock and see him staring at his computer screen, a calculator in hand.

"Greg, I'm going to close the shop," I tell him quietly. He turns around, and I'm shocked by how red his eyes are.

"Thanks, Autumn." He yawns and stretches out his arms. "Honestly, I don't know what this place would do without you." He gives me a small smile.

"I'm thankful for this job," I tell him, but immediately

regret it. I don't want him to feel guilty or anything if Price's can't stay open.

"You know, I've wanted to run a business ever since I was little," he says and puts his arms behind his head.

"Why?" I ask, thinking that's a weird job for a little kid to want. He swivels back and forth on his chair.

"My dad was a businessman. He gave his life to the companies he worked for. He made it seem like it was so honorable, like he was a modern day hero." Greg laughs bitterly at this, and I wait for him to say more. "The prick was never home." He smiles at me, and I can feel his pain.

"Well, you will be," I say, even though Greg doesn't have kids, and the shop might not stay afloat. It doesn't matter. We learn from our parent's mistake and notice what they did wrong so that we can change the cycle. "Not being like your dad isn't a bad thing." I put my hand on his arm and turn him around so that he's facing the computer. "Goodnight, Greg."

"Night, Autumn." He waves after me.

When I arrive home it's late, and I'm tired, but I decide to give my dad a call since we haven't talked in a while. He picks up on the third ring.

"Autumn, I'm glad you called." His voice is loud and enthusiastic. "How are you doing?" he asks.

"I'm well, Dad. How are you?" I start to make a sandwich and hold the phone between my ear and shoulder.

"I'm good. I have some news to tell you." He pauses to cough.

"Okay, go on," I say. My heart jumps and I stop what I'm doing to sit down at the table.

"I made a pretty big decision." He pauses, and I wait for him to continue. "I'm going away. Leaving the area for a while. I don't know when I'll be back," He says the words quickly, and it takes a second before they register.

"Oh." My stomach drops slightly at the thought of the distance between us growing even further when we already only talk over the phone. "Where are you going?"

"Alaska. I leave tomorrow."

"What made you do this?" I guess I shouldn't be surprised. My father has always been familiar with the door.

"I need a new perspective," he says slowly. "After everything that's happened, I think this will help me deal with it all." He's quiet, and I know he wants me to say something.

"Honestly, Dad." I pause and take a deep breath. "If this is what you need." I'm too worn down to argue with him. There's no control I have over the situation, and it's not like his absence can extend any further.

"I'll miss you, Autumn." He coughs, and I wait for him to clear his throat.

"Be careful," I say.

"I will, I love you."

"I love you too," I tell him and then hang up the phone. It's a lot to take in all at once, but deep down I'm almost relieved to cut him away, like a rotting limb—I was attached to him because I needed him and I loved him, but I can survive fine without him.

I think of Greg back at his office as I eat my sandwich. What would he do as a Dad if his kid got sick? It's difficult to imagine. I have nothing against Greg, but it's hard to see how anyone could handle cancer positively when my family failed so miserably. It almost seems like you'd have to be a psycho path, but then, I'm incredibly biased.

CHAPTER 9

As THE WEEKS pass by May and I find more and more time to spend with each other. On the days I don't have work in the morning I sleep over her house, and we waste away the nights in each other's arms whispering stories about when we were younger. May even visits me at Price's if she goes for a walk.

We've been spending so much time together it feels like we've created our own little world. A world that I can actually manage living in.

"Are you alright?" May calls down to me. She's higher up on the trail than I am but not by far.

"I'm just going easy, so I don't embarrass you," I yell to her. I zip my flannel jacket up higher and use the base of a tree to pull myself onto the next level of the dirt path. Since it's the end of October the fall wind is a little rough. This isn't the best day for a hike, but if we waited any longer we'd be making the trip in the snow. The trail isn't too bad, but I'm a little rusty on my outdoor skills. May is like a damn monkey swinging from the tree branches. I guess she used to do this kind of stuff all the time.

"Is that why you're so out of breath?" May grabs my hand

and pulls me along. Even through the briskness the sun is still out, and it's actually a pleasant day. Every time the wind shakes the trees a shower of leaves fall down on us, and we try to catch as many as we can before they hit the ground. I'm able to grab a few from the air, and May gives me all of hers. I bring the dead leaves to my face and inhale them, enjoying fall's freshness. Sometimes dying is endearing.

"I'm always out of breath when I'm with you," I say, and May sticks out her tongue. I try to grab it, but she runs away further up the trail. I attempt to chase after her but trip and fall over a root.

"You okay?" May bends down and while her eyes scan my body for damage, I grab her arm and wrestle her underneath me. "That's no fair. I thought you were really hurt."

I soften my grip, feeling bad for pulling such a cheap move, but then May bucks her hips and flips us over. We tumble through the leaves together until I finally regain my position on top.

"You may be better at climbing mountains, but I can still take you." I plant a quick kiss on her nose and jump up.

"I have to let you win at something," May says, smiling.

When we reach the highest point I pull out a blanket and sprawl it out on the grass. I take out a water bottle from my backpack, give it to May, and pull out a sketchbook for myself.

"I'm taking a nap. Wake me when you're done." May leans back on the blanket and closes her eyes. The breeze carries her hair across her face. I brush the strand behind her ear and touch her lips with my fingers. She smiles and tries to kiss them before I pull away. We stay on the mountain for a few hours which is more than enough time for me to capture a few landscapes.

The way down is easier in essence, but requires more

grace to not fall. May holds my hand the entire time, and we make it back to my car in one piece. It's a little warmer in lower altitude, so we unzip our jackets. The hot chocolate I brought in my mother's old thermos is more for pleasure now than necessity.

"Are you going trick or treating tonight?" I ask, blowing on the liquid. May laughs.

"I wasn't planning on it. Are you?" she asks.

"No, I'd rather give out candy." My mom won't be up late enough to entertain the trick or treaters, and I don't want them to pass by my house again. Besides, I have a lot of discounted candy from Price's. I'm giving away handfuls this year. "Want to help? We can watch scary movies."

"Sounds like we're going to have fun," Mays says, wrapping her arms around my waist.

"I like that we're a 'we.' It makes me feel like you're my partner," I say. May stares at me and smiles slowly.

"I am your partner," she murmurs, and I kiss her once more before I start the car.

When we get back to my house I send May up to my room while I check on my mom. She's sitting at the kitchen table watching the news. She's still in her pajamas, but the sudden interest in current events is a great sign.

"Someone called for you today," she says without turning away from the television. I open up the fridge and take out two apples.

"Did they leave a name?" No one's ever really tried contacting me on our landline, so it seems a little strange.

"It was Mrs. Nelson, your guidance counselor. She wanted to know why you haven't tried meeting with her yet to discuss your college options." My mother's voice is strained and even a little bitter. Unless I'm imagining it, it sounds like she's mad.

"Oh," I say. My mother continues staring at the television.

"Do you have any future plans?" she asks. I move into her line of vision and look down at her.

"Maybe in a few years I'll be promoted to manager of Price's. If I'm motivated enough maybe they'll even let me handle the accountant work," I say sarcastically. She's not amused and remains looking down at the floor. I shuffle awkwardly past her and go upstairs. If Mrs. Nelson wanted to meet with me why couldn't she have just looked for me at school?

"Everything alright?" May asks and takes the apple I hand her. We sit on my bed, and I bite into the tart, red fruit.

"How are we supposed to know what to do with the rest of our lives right now? I feel like I'm not even a complete person yet," I say, and May nods her head knowingly.

"It's kind of anti-climactic, isn't it? You have to spend all this time learning so many different subjects, just to commit your whole life to one profession."

"It's not fair," I say and look at May. "What would you do though? Like if you could be anything."

"There's a lot I wouldn't mind doing, but I guess if I could pick anything I'd live on a tiny ranch with my own garden and farm," May says slowly, her hand rubbing her chin. She looks me in the eye and smiles. "What about you?"

"It doesn't matter." I stopped day dreaming about my future after Mya died. There's nothing that I can do while my mother's still sick. "I'll probably be right here, so when you get your ranch you'll know where to send the postcard." I smile back at May, but she frowns slightly, and I look away.

"I think deep down you know what you want, Autumn," she says and places her hand on my chest. "You just have to be okay with it." I take her hand between my fingers and kiss each of her knuckles.

"Your skin is so soft," I say, nibbling the side of her hand. May giggles, and I lightly bite her.

"Ow!" She pulls away.

"I forgot to tell you." I push my shoulders up and lift my arms straight ahead of me. "On Halloween I turn into a zombie," I say, deepening my voice into my best undead impression. I chase May around the bed, and she screams. I jump on her and start to nibble at the base of her neck. "Mmm flesh," I mumble.

"I don't like it when you're a zombie," May cries, and she sticks out her bottom lip. I look into her watery, surrendering eyes and start to kiss all the spots I bit. May throws her arms around my neck, and I suddenly feel very hot leaning over her on my bed. She pulls me forward and takes my earlobe in between her teeth, biting it hard, and then sucking gently. My hands run up her sides, and I thumb each of the bones in her rib cage. The ringing of the doorbell causes us both to jump and turn towards the hallway.

"My mom's still up, she'll get it." I lean forward to kiss May on the lips, but the bell rings again. "She probably went to bed early," I mumble, giving May a crooked smile. She sits up and pushes us both off the bed.

"Well, we can't leave those little kids waiting." She squeezes my hand, and I can tell that she's excited. Downstairs I quickly open three huge bags of candy and empty the sugary stuff into a giant bowl. When we open the door, we're greeted by a ghost, a princess, and a pirate. I let them all take little handfuls, and they run away to their parents who stand at the edge of my front lawn.

"American culture is so funny sometimes," May says as we watch the little kids sprint to the next house.

"Because we give out free candy?" I put a chocolate bar in her hand, and she smiles, nodding her head.

I set up a scary movie in the living room, and we sit on the couch waiting for more trick- or-treaters. Last year we didn't really get that many people. Mya was locked in her room after the transplant, and I guess the community didn't want to bother us. I bought candy to give out, but we just stayed up late eating all of it until we were sick enough to never indulge in sugar again.

After about two hours of getting up and answering the door May rests on the couch next to me, and the television volume is muted. It's nearly the end of the night, and the spaces between each group of children increase. By now all the little kids are home getting ready for bed, and all the older ones are out. I can hear cars honking through the open window, and I'm sure some type of mischief is going on. I'm just about to turn off the front porch light when the bell rings again. I grab the bowl of candy and open the door, greeted by four kids who look only a few years younger than me. Two of them aren't even in costumes. I hold out the bowl, and they grab the candy quickly but hesitate before leaving. I arch an eyebrow, questioning their remaining presence until one of the boys looks up at me.

"Is this house haunted?" he asks, his voice hitching with puberty. The other three boys wait patiently for my response, but I'm confused by the question.

"Why would my house be haunted?" There are a few old houses in town that people have sworn they've seen ghosts in, but mine isn't one of them.

"Well, it's just that…" The first boy stutters and his friend steps in.

"Someone in your family died here, right?" His voice is confident and even a little harsh. I shake my head slowly, staring each of them down in turn.

"No, no one died here," I say and walk back into my

house. I shut the door and lock it behind me. Sometimes living in a small town has its setbacks.

"All done for the night?" May asks, snaking her arms around my waist and pulling me into her. When I don't melt in her embrace she stares into my eyes, and I look away. "You have to stop doing that," she says.

"Doing what?" I look back up at her.

"You try to hide from me whenever something's bothering you," May says, softly. I cast my gaze down again but immediately snap it back up, offering May a sheepish smile.

"I'm sorry, May." I rub my hand against the back of my neck and try hard not to break eye contact.

"Don't be sorry, just talk to me. I can tell when you're hurting in here." May pokes where my heart is, and I sink backwards, grabbing my chest with both hands.

"Sometimes I just miss my sister," I say quietly. "And my father," I add. May waits for me to say more, but what's left to describe this pain? Sometimes it's just as simple as that. It's as simple as longing for a loved one who doesn't exist anymore.

"Come on, Autumn. Let's go lay down." May cups my hand and leads me up the stairs. In bed I lie on my back, and May rests her head in the crook of my arm, curled into my body. I stroke her bare shoulder lightly with the tips of my fingers and stare up at the ceiling. The darkness goes in and out in splotches, and I squint my eyes to try and adjust to the lack of light.

May wiggles her hand under my shirt and rests it on my stomach. Her fingers are warm, and they feel good against my skin. I take deep breaths, trying to relax and close my eyes, but I'm not tired. When Mya was in a lot of pain I'd draw shapes on her back until she fell asleep. She said it was soothing. I slept in her room a lot when she was in remission.

She had to be hooked up to a big machine that was always pumping medicine into tubes coming out of her chest. I guess the tubes were a lot more convenient than having to stick a needle in her arm 20 times a day. She could never get them wet though, so bathing was hard for her. Not that she could ever wash the smell of sickness from her skin anyway; Mya always smelt like the hospital, even when she was home.

I can't help the memories that reel through my mind like movie clips. I try to think of how it was before Mya got sick, when we'd play cards for hours on summer days or when our whole family played basketball together. We were completely different people back then. Everyone changed so much towards the end. So many dramatic things happened that it's sometimes hard to remember what's real or not.

One time when Mya was back from the hospital she wanted us to watch a movie together, spend time as a family. It was an activity that required the bare minimum of contact. Things were so tense with my parents hating each other though. We couldn't decide on a movie and after ten minutes of discussing our options my father started snapping the DVDs I said I didn't like. My mother cried, so did Mya. After that we stopped trying to do things as a family, and Mya stopped asking us to. We couldn't even keep it together to appease this one request.

I was mad at my dad for the longest time after that. In some ways I hated him, and I even hated that I hated him. I can't help it. I know that it was a hard time for everyone and when I think of how Mya cried, how she held onto his hand when she was dying, I think I should forgive him. Because there's nothing worse than a broken man hovering over the lifeless body of his little girl.

"Are you okay?" May's voice startles me, and I pull away from her slightly. She sits up on the bed and looks down at me. "You're crying," she says, using the corner of the blanket to wipe away my tears.

"I'm sorry," I mumble, drying my eyes clean. I shake my head and try to ground myself in what's happening in front of me. "I was just thinking about the past."

May leans her back against the headboard and gently rests my head in her lap. She strokes my hair away from my face and starts to hum a folk tune.

"The first time I looked at a girl and realized that I was attracted to her, I ran home and cried. She was in the school-yard playing soccer with the boys, and I liked the way she smiled. When she was walking back to the classroom I told her she was beautiful, and she called me a lesbian," May says, quietly.

"How old were you?" I ask, moving my head so that I'm staring up at her.

"I was seven. After that none of the girls would play with me. They'd all run away, scared I might try to kiss them. It didn't last long, but it was upsetting enough, and when I came home crying my mom found me hiding underneath my bed. She pulled me out, laid me in her lap just like this, and played with my hair. She told me I was normal and that everything would be alright."

"Was everything alright?" I ask, playing with her ear. She smiles down at me, but her eyes look like they're holding onto a sadness stirred when discussing things better left forgotten.

"Darling, I think you already know the answer to that," May says and kisses me gently. I wrap my arms around her waist, and she lies further down on the bed so that my head rests on her stomach.

"You're my best friend," I mumble, and she puts her hand inside the back of my shirt to rub my skin. The gesture is so comforting I can't help the sobbing that soon occurs. She keeps rubbing me and hums the old folk song again. I shut my eyes tightly together, trying to hold in tears, but they fall in huge droplets on May's shirt.

"It's okay, Autumn," she says soothingly.

"I know. It just doesn't feel like it's okay," I choke out, gasping for air through my cries.

"I'm going to help you," she whispers.

"How?" My body is so heavy, and I feel pathetic the way I'm slobbering all over May. I lift my head up, but she pushes me back down.

"Get some rest now, darling. You'll see tomorrow," she says, running her fingers up the back of my neck to caress my eyebrow.

"I love you, May," I say and manage to stop my body from shaking.

"I know, Autumn. I love you too."

CHAPTER 10

I MANAGE to sleep a few hours before waking up next to a drool puddle on May's chest. She shifts underneath me, and I sit up slowly, allowing her to turn on her side. I rub my eyes and wince at how irritated they feel.

"You really are a zombie," May mumbles into a pillow. She yawns and stretches out her arms.

"I'm sorry. You can keep sleeping." I watch as May blinks her eyes a couple of times and looks around the room.

"At least the sun is out. I don't need sleep anyway." She smiles at me and gives me a good morning kiss.

"Everyone needs sleep," I say and kiss her back.

"Apparently you don't." May pulls me down on the bed, and we face each. She rubs her thumb along the corner of one of my eyes and offers me a small smile.

"Get some more rest. I'm going downstairs to check on my mom." I plant a kiss on her forehead and walk out of the room, closing the door behind me. The house is pretty cold, so I turn up the thermostat and look outside. Even though it's early the clouds are bunched together in a light flurry.

I go to the kitchen and splash some cold water over my

eyes and face. It wakes me up enough to hear my mother talking in the other room. I walk down the hall and open her bedroom door quietly. She's still lying down and her blankets are twisted in a bunch at the bottom of her bed. I walk over to her slowly and gently touch her shoulder. She jumps at the contact and turns to me, her eyes wild.

"Autumn, you scared me," she says, putting a hand to her chest. I smile slightly because my name came to her lips immediately, but she looks like she had a rough night.

"Are you okay?" I ask her, putting the back of my hand to her forehead. She feels pretty warm, and I can tell by the tissues lying around her nightstand that she's probably getting sick.

"I'm fine," she says and purses her lips into a straight line. I look around the bed. There's no phone or any device used to verbally communicate.

"Who were you talking to?" My mother looks away from me and pulls at the blankets.

"No one," she whispers. I grab the blankets off the bed and throw them on the floor. They need to be washed anyway and so do the sheets. Before my mother opens her mouth to protest I put a finger over her lips.

"You're getting a fever. You need to go upstairs and take a hot shower. I'll change your bedding." My voice is full of authority, and she doesn't question my commands. I watch as she drags herself out of the bed and through the door. Her sheets haven't been cleaned in a while, and I feel a little bad for not thinking to wash them before.

When she comes out of the shower I make up the couch with some clean linen and a wool blanket. I make her a hot cup of tea and put on the television. She takes a sip of the liquid, and I go back to the kitchen to make us all something to eat. Even though my mother hasn't parented me lately, I don't know what I'd do if I lost her. The thought causes anxiety to boil in my chest. I try to focus on the stove and crack a few eggs into a frying pan.

I don't go back upstairs until my mother has eaten every single bite off her plate. I stand over her with my arms crossed around my chest and wait patiently. She doesn't say anything the whole time, but when she's done I bring her plate to the kitchen and tuck her tightly into the wool blanket. Her eyes follow me, but I can't look into them because I think she might feel bad, and I'd rather not recognize that.

When I open my bedroom door May stirs slightly, but it isn't until I kiss the back of her neck that she opens her eyes. I place the plate of eggs in front of us, and we eat together quietly.

"Want me to help you rake the leaves today?" she asks, and I nod my head, offering her a smile. It's a chore I've been putting off for the last couple of weeks since we've been hanging out. With the cold and the possible rain, it'll be harder to do any later than today. We get dressed quickly, and I give May something of mine to wear.

To my relief my mother's on the couch fast asleep. Hopefully she'll feel better by tomorrow because I really don't know how I'd drag her to the doctor. May follows me out the front door, and I grab a rake and a huge tarp from the shed to carry the leaves on. I don't really want May to do any of the hard work, so I give her a blanket to sprawl out on the ground and start raking leaves into piles. It takes a little less than two hours to do the front lawn. I look up at the oak tree, now practically bare.

May throws down the blanket and runs towards the tree, jumping on the tire swing that hangs from the lowest branch. I run up behind her and give the swing one big push. It was Mya's idea to make the swing back when we were in junior high. She found a tire on the side of the road and rolled it back to our house one day after school. Before our parents got home we were able to successfully find a rope strong enough to hold the weight and attach it to the tree. Jamie had to help us because even though I could climb up to the branch, he knew how to tie the knot so that it was safe. My mother pulled into the driveway and jumped out of her car before it was even put in park to force us off the "death trap." It was only after my dad inspected the swing that we were allowed back on.

I push May one more time before jumping on the other side and swing my legs over the rope. She holds onto my shoulders and leans into me. The branch dips with our weight and May yelps. I manage a chuckle because even with Mya, Jamie, and I riding the swing at the same time the branch never broke. Of course, that was a few years ago, but if anything, the tree has gotten stronger over time, and I have a lot of faith in Jamie's knot.

"Are you feeling better today?" May asks, her lips touch my ear before she leans back, elevating the swing higher. I push forward, and we work together to move the swing back and forth.

"I guess so," I say, but the pain is still there. It's just a game of keeping the top screwed on a shaken soda bottle. Before May, I had such a solid grip on the cap, but lately it feels so good to let some seep out.

"It broke my heart to see your tears last night." May watches me, and I tilt my head down. I shouldn't have cried like that. "Autumn, what did I tell you about hiding from me?" She gives me a small smile and nudges my chin up so that I'm facing her.

"I'm sorry," I say quickly. I can feel my cheeks burn, and

even though May's hand keeps my chin up, I avoid looking in her eyes.

"What do you have to be embarrassed about?" May asks, her voice softening.

"I'm just such a mess. There's so much inside me that I can't let go of. I feel like I'm a burden, like one of those friends you have to put up with," I mumble, and May lets go of me. She steps off the tire swing and stands next to me.

"Autumn, other kids our age cry about not getting the dress they want for prom. Your problems are a little more intricate than that." May gives me a sideways smile. "I love you, darling. You're not a burden to me. You're good company to weather a storm with," she says and wraps her arms around my waist, pulling me off of the swing. She kisses me, and I try to push away my insecurities.

"I just worry that I'm too much sometimes." I think of my mother on the couch and my sister's empty bedroom. "You've been nothing but kind to me," I say, and May cocks her eyebrows.

"And I'll keep being kind to you because I love you." May kisses me again, silencing the conversation.

"Let's go inside. I'll make us some tea." I grab May's hand, and she slides her fingers through mine. In the kitchen, I put water in the kettle and set it on the stove. May sits on one of the counter stools, and I look over at my mother still asleep. I put two slices of bread in the toaster for her to eat when she wakes up, and take out a container of jam.

"You'd be a great mom," May says while watching me. I let out a loud laugh.

"I do not want kids." I shake my head at the thought of being responsible for another human being. I can barely handle my own issues.

"You might change your mind when you're older." May shrugs.

"I think we both know that I'm not capable of something like that," I say and wink at her. She shakes her head at me, and I set my mother's food down on the coffee table for when she wakes.

"Did you and Mya ever play tea time?" May asks. I put a hot mug in front of her.

"All the time, but I hated it. Mya only got me to stay seated for 10 minutes at a time before I dragged her outside," I say, smiling at the memory of our backyard adventures.

"It's so strange," May says, looking at me curiously.

"What is?" I add a spoonful of honey to my tea and stir the liquid.

"I can tell you're really happy when you talk about her. You smile wider, your eyes shine brighter, but then your shoulders fall forward, and these lines pull your lips down." May runs her fingers down my cheek where my skin creases. "You're trying to hold onto something that keeps breaking free."

I look into May's eyes and feel comforted by their softness. Is it wrong of me to try to keep Mya with me? I knit my brow together and take a sip of tea.

"I just don't want to forget her," I say steadily. May gently places her hand atop my own.

"You're not going to forget her, Autumn. She's your sister. It's just that, I can tell you're hurting." May's words confuse me, but I hear my mother stir on the couch. I point my finger to the stairs, signaling for May to go up to my bedroom. She nods her head, and my mother sits up and pulls down the heavy blanket.

"How are you feeling?" I ask her, placing a hand to her

forehead. She's still a little warm, but her eyes aren't as fogged up as they were this morning.

"Better," she mumbles. I put the plate of toast on her lap and tell her to eat. She nods her head and takes a nibble of the bread. I pour her a cup of orange juice and leave her the remote control to entertain herself. She'll probably feel better by tomorrow.

I go upstairs and into my room. I sit down next to May on the bed and rest my head against her shoulder. She rubs my back softly, and I moan as her fingers touch me.

"It does hurt, May," I say quietly. "But I don't think it'll ever go away." I feel May's arm slide away, and she stands up in front of me. She pulls me up and kisses me hard on the mouth. I pull back and look into gentle blue eyes.

May bows her head so that her breath tickles my neck. She squeezes me closer, and her strong arms, like branches, keep me from falling as my knees lose their power to support. Her lips are soft and warm against my skin, leaving bulletless holes burning into me. She shoots me a few more times before I capture the barrel in my mouth and bite down gently. May puts the palm of her hand on my chest, directly above my heart, and I know she can feel each beat pound against her. I wrap my hands around the small of her back right before it arches and pull her into me. I want to feel her skin against my skin, her fingers tangled in my hair, but still, it doesn't seem like even that would be enough. May pushes her hand harder into my chest.

"I can make it go away," she whispers in my ear and tucks two fingers into the rim of my jeans. The air in my lungs evaporates, and my heart swells at the possibility of a release. The weight is so heavy it drags me forward, and I think I might faint. May sits me on the bed. I grab my chest with both hands and breathe in heavily.

"Darling, it's going to be okay." May kisses my cheek, and I can feel her eyelashes tickle my skin. I nod my head and try to relax. I take May's hand and kiss each of her fingers. She stands up in front of me and pushes my shoulders back on the bed so that I'm lying down. "I'll be right back." She kisses me quick on the lips, and I listen to her walk out of the room and down the hall. I close my eyes and resist the urge to follow her. I try not to think of anything. I push my eyelids harder together and focus on the splotches of color. I hear water running in the bathroom.

I stand up and open the window to air out the heat that's gathered in the room. The sky's in a state of hysteria from carrying a storm all day, and it seems that at any moment it'll rain. If it's cold enough, it might even hail. I open the window screen and stick my head through the hole, allowing my hair to tangle in the wind, my eyes to water. The feeling in my face makes it harder to numb the beating in my chest. In fact, never in my life have I wanted to scream any louder, but the wildness in the air turns my anxiety into excitement, and I actually believe that tonight I will heal.

"Autumn." May tugs me back into the bedroom. "What are you doing?" She laughs at my knotted hair and red cheeks.

"It's beautiful outside," I tell her, helplessly attempting to run my fingers through the tangled mess atop my head.

"It's quite amazing." May takes a step forward and looks out the window. I put my hands under the back of her shirt and warm my cold fingers against her hot skin. I can feel the bones of her vertebrae go rigid against my coolness, but she doesn't pull away. I lift her shirt up higher and kiss one of the bones below her neck. I hear her breathe in harshly as I slowly snake my fingers around her rib cage. The wind blows into the room, and May turns around to hide her face from its wrath. I close the window, and an empty silence fills the room as if a great presence has suddenly left.

"I'm going to help you." May cups my hand in hers and escorts me to the hallway.

"Help me with what?" I ask. May leads me into the bathroom and locks the door behind us.

"Autumn, I can make the pain go away," she says again, and I feel dizzy.

"How?" I ask in a whisper. It amazes me that she even understands my pain. She has a perfect family, all alive and healthy. She's barely an adult, but she's seen the world already, or at least a lot of it. She can't relate to my empty life, but she did notice it. I can't believe how easily she understands what I've gone through. It's like she can see the imprint of my sister and father and where they used to be. Like if one day you rearranged the furniture in a living room and all the marks of where the couches and chairs once were, remained impressed in the carpet. May noticed the empty spaces and the marks on the floor immediately. I guess anyone who knew about my life and cared enough to think about it would've noticed the same, but it's harder to recognize the actual feeling of an empty room. Not without being able to relate.

May kisses me lightly on the lips and then slowly lifts her shirt over her head. I've seen girls change plenty of times before but never like this. I've never watched like this either. May smiles at me and unhooks her bra. I've never been in front of a naked woman before, and the nerves are enough to make my hands shake. May seems perfectly comfortable though, and, without hesitation, she discards the rest of her clothing into a neat pile on the white tile floor. Her long hair falls in front of her shoulders. She brushes it up into a bun, and then points to the bathtub. I forgot she'd been running water and just now notice the tub is full.

"I find that healing happens best with water," May says, gripping the bottom of my shirt so she can pull it easily over my head. I suppose she's right. The river has always comforted me, even on the worst nights.

May pulls me in close to her and kisses behind my ear while unhooking my bra. It falls to the floor between us, and I gasp as her bare skin touches mine. My chest swells up as it did before, and my jaw locks right as I kiss May's collar. I bite down harder than expected, but May doesn't wince even though I'm sure it'll leave a bruise. My cheeks are hot as I feel her against me. She unbuttons my pants, and I try to gracefully shake out of them, but May bends down and pulls each leg off of my feet. She kisses up my thighs. I stand rigid in front of her, feeling paralyzed by my emotions. She pulls down my underwear and takes hold of my hand.

"It's going to be okay," she whispers in my ear, and I step into the tub. The water is hot so we lower ourselves into it slowly. We sit facing each other and stretch out our legs. May pulls me closer to her so that I'm sitting on her lap, and I wrap my legs around her waist. I can't stop putting my lips on her skin. I want to make us one with my mouth. I want to swallow her, to feel her beating in my chest, and to have her conquer everything inside of me. Maybe she'll even quench my thirst.

"You love me?" I ask her because I need to hear it right now.

"I love you, Autumn," she says, her hands running up my breasts gently, like a quiet wave washing over a smooth stone. It feels good, and I open my mouth to kiss her, but May touches me, and I pull away.

"I don't know how to do this," I say. May smiles and turns me around so that I lean back against her chest.

"It's okay. I'm going to show you." Her fingers dance up my thighs, and her lips press against the back of my neck. She touches me slowly, cupping me in the palm of her hand. Even though she's gentle what she touches causes me to jolt back and moan at the same time.

"Shhh, it's okay," May whispers in my ear. She turns on the shower extension that's fallen into the tub, adjusting it so the water shoots out in a quick rhythmic pattern and spreads my legs apart underneath her own. Her fingers are in my hair caressing my scalp; they move down my neck and up again in repeated succession. Her breath in my ear is soothing and I release the air I was holding out into the steam around us. I relax into her, close my eyes, and feel the water beating against me. It tingles at first, but I learn how to grasp at the sense of pleasure like a child chasing a butterfly. Almost catching the beauty but letting it go quicker and quicker. It becomes too much to merely grasp anymore. I clench onto the feeling and hold on for as long as I can, but the sensation escalates, climaxes, and I have to release. I fall into an explosion—a warm, wet fire as everything in my body burns away only to be superseded by waves of pleasure. I gasp into the hot, moist air, pushing the shower extension away. May drops it to the bottom of the tub. My body curls into her.

"Are you alright?" May's voice sounds far away, I can barely hear it. I press my face into her chest, confirming she's right here in front of me. May starts to hum, and I sink further into the water so that it covers me like a blanket. I feel the heaviness creep up the back of my neck, and my body falls limp. Through my stiff lips I manage to mumble 'thank you.' I hold onto her, but I can't stay awake any longer. I need to sleep.

CHAPTER 11

I WAKE up in my bed naked and alone. The clock illuminates 4:07am. I jump up and run to the bathroom. My clothes are still on the floor, but May's are gone, and the tub is drained. She must've carried me to bed and went home. That's impossible though. May has some strength to her but not enough to lift my unconscious body down the hallway. Maybe I was half awake or something. I just don't remember anything past being in the bathtub. I can't believe May left. It's not like she hasn't slept over before, and after what happened in the tub it would've been nice if she was still next to me when I woke. What am I saying? I'm just being needy. What was she supposed to do anyway? Watch me sleep?

I pick my clothes up off the floor and bring them to my room. I toss them in the laundry basket next to my bed and notice something sticking out from underneath my mattress. I slowly pull it out and notice that it's the picture of Mya in the hospital after her transplant. I smile slightly at the sight of my sister's face and rub my finger along her cheek. I gently place the picture back under my mattress and dress quickly into my usual jeans, t-shirt, and cardigan attire.

When I go down the stairs my mother's in the kitchen making tea. There's a collection of tissues spilling out of her sweater pocket, but she looks better.

"You're up early." I pull out a box of cereal from the cabinet along with a bowl and a spoon.

"I couldn't sleep." She hands me milk from the fridge. "Do you want any?" She points to the steam covered kettle, and I shrug my shoulders. She takes out another mug and pours us each a cup. I sit across from her at the table and eat my cereal.

"How are you feeling?" I take in her combed hair, her red nose, and the slight color to her cheeks.

"Better than those poor guys." I look up and see that she's pointing out the window to a nest holding four baby birds sitting on the tree in our front lawn. They aren't screaming, but they do look cold. It seems like a strange time of year for bird babies to be born. The air gets colder by the day.

"That's rough," I say and look away from them.

"You know, when you were little you used to save everything. We weren't even allowed to kill spiders." My mom looks at me and smiles.

"I don't remember that. Are you sure it wasn't Mya?" I almost regret saying her name, but my mom's reaction is normal. She shakes her head and closes her eyes.

"It was definitely you. I can still remember you trying to herd all the ants out of the house when your father would try to squish them." She looks at me, and I can tell she wants me to have a moment of recognition from the memory, but I don't. I take another bite of my cereal.

"Sorry, Mom, I must've been too young to remember." She blows at her tea and shrugs.

"I guess so." She smiles at me softly, and I think she still might be thinking of me as a little kid. "I'm going to lay down. Have a good day at school."

"Thanks," I say, and she walks back into her room. I finish my cereal and peer out the front window. I look outside and press my hand against the glass. The coldness makes me feel grounded and alive. I want more of it. A walk will help me gather myself and clear my head before the busy day. I grab my coat and slip on my old worn boots. The air is so dry and harsh that when I first breathe in it makes me cough.

I think of last night and a warm heat rushes between my legs. I felt so safe leaning against May while her arms were around me, her hands holding my existence together and yet making me burst open. For the first time since I can remember, life seems beautiful. I smile to myself at the thought. It sounds ridiculous, but I didn't know that I could feel this way. I'd forgotten.

I take my hands out of my coat pocket and stretch my fingers, grasping at the air. A few snowflakes mill about, not really settling but frosting over the sidewalk. I hear heavy footsteps behind me and turn around.

"Hey, Autumn," Jamie says through heavy breaths. The tips of his ears are almost as red as his hair, and I can see air exhaling from his mouth.

"Isn't it a bit early for a run?" I ask, noticing his worn sneakers and hope that he's wearing two pairs of socks.

"Isn't it a bit early for a walk?" He smiles at me, and I see his point. We start walking together as Jamie stretches.

"So are you playing football in college?" I ask, mainly because I have no idea what his future plans are.

"You're funny, Autumn." Jamie chuckles. "My mom would kill me. It was hard enough convincing her to let me play varsity." I forgot that football was actually potentially dangerous.

"True," I say, nodding my head. "How will the team fair next year without you?" Regardless of his mother's worries, he's one of the best athletes at our school.

"Actually, they won't have to." For a moment I think he's kidding, but the look on his face is serious.

"Why not?" I ask, and we stop for a minute so Jamie can stretch his quads.

"Haven't you heard?" There's sweat marks under his arms, and I know he'll be colder in a few minutes. The thought makes me shiver.

"About what?"

"The football program got cut." We stop walking, and I turn to Jamie. I have no interest in sports, but it's something Jamie enjoyed so much. I feel sorry for him. I offer him a small smile and grab his hand when he puts his foot down. He smiles, and I squeeze his fingers lightly.

"I'm sorry, Jamie." He gives me a small squeeze back, and I let go. I think back to Jamie's first game. It feels like a lifetime ago. Mya and I went together to watch him with a couple of her friends who had crushes on other, slightly older, players. It was a few months before Mya got sick, one of the last 'normal' nights before my life was consumed by hospital visits. Jamie made varsity our freshmen year. He's a natural athlete, or it's just a small school, but still, he stood out. During that game he scored a touchdown, out-running two players from the other team. The crowd went crazy. I remember seeing a few more of his games after that, but once Mya got sicker I stopped going.

"Can the team fundraise money to keep the program?" I ask, immediately thinking of all the fundraising the town did for Mya.

"It's rough, Autumn. Football wasn't the only program cut. The budget wasn't passed last spring, so a lot of the "extra" stuff is going too. Say goodbye to drama, band, and art."

"The art classes were cut?" I'm surprised by how much the thought saddens me.

"To be honest, I don't know. My mom's on the board, but she doesn't tell me much. I think they're having trouble deciding what to do."

"Are you sure football is getting cut then?" I ask, hoping his answer isn't definite. He looks at me sideways, and we start walking again.

"Last week after dinner one night, my mom set a brand new laptop in front of me."

"What!" Jamie's mother was always so strict with gifts. Even on Christmas he'd only get socks and one item from his wish list.

"Yeah, I thought she was going crazy or something. Then I realized it was a pity gift. We haven't talked about it, but it makes sense. Football only serves half the school's population at most since girls don't play, and I'm sure the whole liability issue with kids possibly getting hurt added an incentive." I can understand that logic but still feel bad. Jamie does a little hop, and I can tell he's starting to feel the cold.

"You should start running again and warm up." I smile and give him an encouraging push.

"The temperature does feel like it dropped 10 degrees. I'll see you at school." He waves and jogs off. I turn around and head for home.

The day goes by quickly. I don't see May at all, even in the classes we have together. I want to stop by her house and check in on her before work but know that it's an unlikely feat when, at the end of English class, Ms. Rogan takes a phone call and tells me to go to the guidance counselor's office. Mrs. Nelson has finally gotten a chance to try and push some direction out of me.

Her office smells like Chinese food, and there's a smudge of black sauce below her lower lip. Why do guidance counselors seem so disorganized? It's like the biggest oxymoron. However, looking at her messy desk compared to my clean house does make me feel slightly better about my own life.

"Hello, Autumn. I'm so happy I got a hold of you. Do you have a few minutes?" She brushes a stack of manila folders to the edge of her desk so we can see each other fully.

"I have to be at work soon," I tell her.

"I'll be quick then." She sits up straight, and I feel like she's about to be strict with me. "I know that you don't have any future plans." It wasn't what I expected her to say. I clear my throat.

"You're right. I don't." Why lie at this point?

"After everything that's happened, no one expects you to have it all figured out." The mention of my past makes my cheeks grow hot. I think she might just want to help, but the conversation immediately makes me uncomfortable. I nod my head and don't say anything.

"I just want you to think about possible options. The Community College accepts admissions into the summer. You could start off there if you want to stay close to home." I know that this is her job, but there's something agitating about a stranger trying to direct your life. Yet, I almost feel bad for her. How do you guide someone who's so lost? I try not to cringe.

"I'll think about it." The stress that comes with the thought overwhelms me, but I offer Mrs. Nelson a smile before I stand and leave to go to work.

. . .

"You seem more relaxed today," Kelvin says while picking at the white plaque between his teeth.

"How so?" I ask, trying not to watch him. We've cleaned the store twice over and are watching cars pass by through the big, empty window.

"I don't know. Maybe you've just been getting more sleep." Kelvin shrugs and wipes the collected white gook on his jeans.

"You know we sell toothbrushes for stuff like that." I try not to sound mean, but I think he's taken aback anyway. "How do you know about me not sleeping anyway?" I change the subject back quickly.

"You usually have huge bags underneath your eyes."

I instinctually touch my face. The skin feels tender beneath my cool finger tips. Kelvin looks tired too, but I let it alone. Outside there's over a dozen birds hanging out in the tree next to our parking lot. All at once they lift off together, shaking the bare branches.

"How do you keep baby birds warm?" I ask him. He looks outside too and watches as the birds settle on another tree in the distance.

"I think the mom sits on them or near them."

"What if they don't have a mom?"

"They're probably screwed then." I think of the baby birds, cold and alone. Even if I was able to keep them warm it's not like I could teach them how to fly. "You could put a heating pack in their nest though."

"Like one of those plastic medical ones?" I ask.

"No, that's too hard." Kelvin scrunches his eyebrows together, and I'm a little surprised he's giving this so much thought. "Take a sock and fill it with rice. Put it in the microwave for a few minutes, and it'll get nice and hot. Then you can place it in the nest, and the baby birds can snuggle right up next to it." Kelvin smiles to himself and then looks at me with his hands tucked into his hips like he's Superman. I give him a playful punch on the shoulder.

"Not bad, problem solver. Where did you come up with that?"

"My mother used to make them for me when I'd get sick as a child."

"She's certainty resourceful," I say, having a hard time imagining Kelvin as a young boy.

"Yeah, I miss that about her." The words leave Kelvin's lips slowly, as if he was unsure he actually wanted to say them. Despite the many hours we've spent alone together we've never really talked about anything too personal.

"Is she dead?" I immediately regret my bluntness, but Kelvin doesn't mind.

"Yeah, car accident when I was 10." He sighs. "I know you know what it's like, to lose someone." He looks at me carefully, and I feel like I'm being inspected. "It was hard at first, but you learn to live with it." I nod my head, trying to show him that I understand what he's saying. "I still miss her." We look at each other, and my lips won't move.

"I know," I say quietly. We watch cars drive by until it's time to close.

When I arrive home I'm not surprised to find my mom asleep on the couch. I put my hand against her forehead, relieved she's not radiating heat. I go into her room, hoping to find one of my father's socks left behind. I open the top drawer of his dresser and shuffle through his old underwear, trying not to think about what I'm touching. I find a long white tube sock and bring it to the kitchen. There's not that much rice left in the cabinet, but I guess I'm lucky we have any at all. I clumsily pour the rest of it in the sock and have to pick a dozen strays off the counter. I tie a knot at the end and put it on a plate in the microwave. I'm not too sure how long to put it in for, so I try a minute. I look outside the window but can't see the nest in the dark. When the microwave beeps the sock is hot, and I have to hold it by the knot.

A small ladder is already next to the tree when I go outside. I step onto it and shine my flashlight over the nest. The baby birds are asleep next to what looks like one of my father's socks stuffed with rice. I gently poke at it to be sure. It's not warm now, but it probably was an hour ago. I think back to this morning, how my mother watched the birds shivering. I look back at the house, and my heart feels heavy. Very carefully I replace her sock heater with mine without waking the birds. Hopefully, they're not already dead.

"It's a little late for tree climbing," a small voice says behind me. I turn around and see May standing a few feet away.

"I thought you skipped town." I climb down from the ladder and walk over to her. She eyes the sock in my hand but doesn't ask.

"I think your mom got me sick. I didn't feel very well today." She tugs at the scarf around her neck to make it tighter. I place my hand against her forehead. She feels warm.

"You probably shouldn't have come out in this cold." I rub my hands against her shoulders.

"I missed you though." She gives me a small kiss on the lips. "Did anything crazy happen when I was gone?"

"The chemistry teacher set off a huge explosion, and half the student body now has blue skin." I smile.

"I guess I'm lucky you didn't get affected, but I think I'd like you blue." She runs her thumb over my brow.

"I found out this morning that a bunch of programs are

getting cut. I guess the school is struggling with money." I think of Price's. "The whole town is struggling with money."

"That's unfortunate." May frowns, and her eyes soften.

"I just wish that there was a way to fix everything." I feel bad for Greg and Jamie and everyone else affected by the lack of financial stability.

"You can try to think of ways to help, darling. Just know that these things take time. It gets better slowly, but it can happen." May starts to cough.

"Let's get you inside."

I tuck her into bed next to me, and she falls asleep almost immediately. I lay awake, thinking of what can be done to help the town, but nothing seems feasible. The weight of the problem puts me into a restless slumber.

CHAPTER 12

THE NEXT FEW weeks fly by quietly. I spend most of my time hiding out in the library because it's the warmest room in the school. I work on sketches as May reads books of poetry next to me. Every once in a while, she'll whisper a line in my ear that makes my cheeks hot. When I wake up in the mornings the frost on the grass grows thicker, as does my breath. Small changes occur. Kelvin starts brushing his teeth. For two weeks my mom attentively reheats the bird heater, until one day the babies aren't in their nest anymore. We find one of them dead on the ground close to the tree.

"Maybe the other two flew away," I say, still looking around for any possible bodies. My mom bends over the bird to examine it.

"Or they also fell and were eaten by other animals." We bury the bird in a small hole near the side of the house. I think of my mom at Mya's grave and swallow hard.

"Fuck it," she says, walking back into the house. I'm so shocked I almost laugh. My mom has never sworn in front of me before. I pat the soil hard over the hole and follow her.

"What do you mean?" I grab her attention before she has time to close the door to her room.

"Just, fuck it," she says simply and shuts the door. Needless to say, the dead birds make for a depressing Thanksgiving. They leave their own hole in my heart that makes me quick to anger. I can't control it. It's as if I'm watching myself interact with the people around me, unable to stop. All of the pain I feel is buried underneath a graveyard of tightly clenched fists, and something inside of me just wants to attack.

"How's your day going?" Kelvin asks, leaning against the counter I just wiped.

"Fine, I suppose." I eye his greasy fingers smudging the plastic and leaving streaks. I take my rag and rub the spot next to his hand.

"Is it just me, or has your OCD gotten more intense lately?" Kelvin backs away from the counter and walks to the end of the store. "I'm going to stock some shelves." He calls out.

"What's the point?" Greg whispers, more to himself than me, as he approaches the counter. "Autumn, can I talk to you in the back?" In all of the time I've spent at Price's, Greg has never asked to have a private conversation with me. The way he avoids eye contact makes me fear the worst. I swallow hard and follow him to his office. We can't both fit in the room, so I stand in the doorway. At first he sits in his chair but then quickly stands up after realizing the limited space.

"So uh, there's something I have to discuss with you." He fidgets slightly, and I nod my head, encouraging him to continue. "You've been a great employee so far, and I really value everything you've done." A sudden sweat rushes over me. My mind panics as I wait for him to fire me.

"I've received a few complaints this month in regards to your customer service. I know that you probably don't mean to be rude, but your attitude isn't like it used to be." Greg doesn't look at me once. I guess it's hard, scolding a girl who lost her sister to cancer.

"I'm sorry, Greg. I'll work on it," I tell him, feeling embarrassed. He nods his head and sits in his chair. I take that as my cue the conversation is over. Back at the counter I turn to Kelvin.

"I know I've been tense lately." I grab my rag and rub at his fingerprints again.

"It's like I'm walking on egg shells, Autumn." I feel him watching me. "Is it something that I did?" he asks quietly. I stop rubbing and shake my head.

"No, Kelvin. I—I can't explain it." He puts his arm on my shoulder, and I ignore the want to shake it off.

"You don't have to. We're friends. You're entitled to some bad days." I smile at him, but my insides shake. I feel like I might be going crazy.

May is waiting for me when I arrive home. She's on the tire swing, swaying gently.

"I hope you haven't been here long. The temperature is dropping." She jumps off the swing and plants a kiss on my lips.

"The cold makes me feel alive, darling." I rub her fingers. They must be numb.

"Well your body feels like a corpse." I bring her inside quickly and make some tea. May leans against the counter, and I can feel her eyes following me. I start to load the dish-washer and hear her come closer to me.

"You're eerily quiet, my love," she says, her lips pressed against my ear, arms snaking around my middle. I sigh and set a cup back in the sink.

"I'm not doing well," I whisper. Her fingers, warmer now, gently scratch my back. "I'm struggling, May," I say quietly. May turns me around and hugs me.

"I know you are. Why don't we talk about it." She smiles softly. May always seems to have an answer. She's so confident and sure of herself. I envy that. I bite my lip.

"What would happen if I took more of you?" I ask, and pull back so I'm looking her in the eye.

"What do you mean?" May quirks an eyebrow. She brushes my hair back with her fingers and it's a comfort I wasn't expecting. I press my head into her hand.

"How much left is there, after you've already given me so much?" I ask.

"There will always be enough." Her words are like a dream and I feel faint.

"Don't you think we should go upstairs?" she asks, and I nod. We go to my bedroom and I strip out of my clothes from the day and put on shorts and an old t-shirt that has holes in the shoulder. May wiggles her fingers into them and sits down next to me on my bed.

"It's not like anger is a stranger to me, but for so long I had that part of me locked up, lying in wait until there was time to process it all," I say. It's an uncomfortable feeling, the rage boiling inside of me. "But now that there's time I don't want it."

Mya had no problem spewing out her rage. I don't blame her, but sometimes it was a little rough, the things she would say. Such harsh, livid words. I knew they all came from pain and fear. She'd cut into me or my mom and dad and we'd just take it. Well, I took it. Most of the time. Fighting would get pretty circular, and there wasn't much wind in my digs. Often she'd make my mother cry though. I'd find her in the bathroom, leaking tears into tissue paper too weak to hold the burden, mumbling about how she was doing her best.

"You were living in constant tension, Autumn." May sinks her fingers into my hair again, and I try not to think about how rough and dirty the strands might feel. "It makes sense that you buried pieces of yourself away."

"I just don't like who I'm becoming," I mumble. My fists tighten against my thighs. All this time I've been so empty and now this, this is what I'm filled with; an unwavering rage.

"You're safe, you know," May says. "No one's dying anymore. You're okay."

We fold into the bed together. May worms herself behind me, holding me against herself, mumbling the same words into my ear, "you're safe, you're safe," until I fall asleep.

In the morning May is gone, but I've gotten used to her not staying the night when I fall asleep. I don't want to leave the comfort of my bed with the cold winter air penetrating the walls outside my bedroom. The sound of music trailing distantly from the kitchen draws me up though. I walk down the stairs to find my mom making pancakes in her old clothes while listening to the radio. An unusual start to a Sunday morning.

"What's the occasion?" My words are quiet, and I'm not sure she hears me at first. She turns around, and I can tell she's wearing mascara as well.

"There's only three weeks left until Christmas, Autumn."

She smiles and flips a pancake. I smile back, suddenly remembering the love my mother has for the holiday. I almost feel excited. The smell of Christmas used to hang from the pine needles in our living room, starting the day after Thanksgiving until someone threw it out, lovingly, a week into the new year. We used to drink hot chocolate and sit by the fire while listening to "Jingle Bells."

"Do you want to get a tree?" The thought pops into my head so quick I don't have time to think twice before I verbalize it. My mom's eyes light up subtly though, and I give her a sideways smile.

"I'd love to." She puts a plate in front of me. I grab a fork and take a bite. I haven't eaten pancakes since Mya was still alive. They were her favorite. It's unsettling seeing my mother move around, not in a funk, but this morning feels different, like life is almost normalizing.

"I'm going to get ready." I go upstairs to shower. In the bathroom, my hand traces over the pencil marks of leaves on the wall before I enter the hot water. Inside, I try to relax as the warmth washes over me. Change is a process; it happens slowly. My rational brain knows this, and it tells me that this isn't permanent, but my mom has been trying. She's just trying a little bit harder today, and now we're getting a Christmas tree. I can't help but smile.

It feels weird handing my mom the keys and sitting in the passenger seat. It's nice not being in control though. We travel to one of the town's farms where a family of 14 grows Christmas trees on their property. There's a dusting of snow at our feet as we search for the perfect pine tree. A boy a few years younger than myself trails behind us with a bow saw. My mom stops before a tree with a slight curve in the middle that straightens out at the tip.

"What do you think of this one?" She nudges me with her

elbow. The tree is in better condition than most in the lot, so I nod.

"It's perfect," I say. My mom points to the tree while addressing the boy. He gets on his knees and starts sawing away. We tie it to the top of her car and drive home. I'm able to drag it to the door mostly by myself, but she takes over the setup process. I didn't notice it before, but there's a box on the living room floor filled with old decorations.

"We have to let it sit so the branches can fluff out before decorating," my mom says after we straighten the tree into a base. I brush the needless off my sweater and look outside. The sun's already setting, but there's enough light to see snow slowly starting to fall. My mom disappears into her bedroom, and I'm worried for a moment until she returns with a glass bottle. She takes out two wine glasses from our cabinet.

"This was your father's favorite. He wasn't much of a drinker, but on the rare occasion he chose to celebrate, this was always his choice." She pours a small sip into one of the glasses and a much larger amount into the other.

"Thanks," I say quietly as she hands me the smaller glass. I've never drunk alcohol before, nor have I had any interest or time to consider the experience. This seems like the perfect occasion though. I "cheers" my mother as she sits down next to me on the couch. We look at the tree, and I take a sip. It's a red wine, leaving my tongue with a taste of something bitter. I'm glad she didn't pour me a bigger glass.

"How's work been?" She drinks, a slight purple staining her upper lip, but avoids making eye contact with me after. I think of the conversation Greg had with me yesterday; it feels like weeks ago. I take another sip of wine.

"It's okay." I tug at a loose string on the hem of my shirt sleeve. "The shop might go out of business."

"That's not a surprise." She shrugs. "It was one of the town's concerns when the Super Center became a neighbor."

"Did anyone boycott or try to stop that from happening?" I ask, not remembering the reaction even though it was only a few years ago.

"There wasn't much we could do. We all said we'd support locally, but the deals are just too strong." My mom gives a bitter laugh, but I fail to see any humor with the image of Greg, sweaty and tired, in his back office.

"There has to be something we can do to help," I say, more to myself than her, but she looks thoughtful anyway. "The football program is getting cut too," I blurt out. Her eyes widen in shock.

"Oh, I wasn't expecting that." She stands up and opens the hatch above the fireplace.

"Yeah, Jamie's pretty upset." I bend down to help her.

"Jamie! How is he?" Black soot covers my hands, and I wipe them on my jeans.

"He seems alright. Do we even have firewood?" I ask. "His mom's going to be a wreck in a few months."

"I'm surprised she's not following him." My mom laughs. "I always thought you two would make a cute couple." Her comment shocks me into silence for a moment.

"I'm glad you're not a matchmaker," I mumble.

"What? He's cute."

"He's practically my brother," I say, my voice heightened. I can't even think of Jamie in a romantic way. My mother goes into the garage to find wood. I think of May, the snowfall, and her numb fingers.

"It's going to be a short fire." My mom comes back with a thin log and a handful of old newspapers. She pours herself another glass of wine, and we set to work building the flames. I try to think of something to ask her, to talk to her about, but

I'm afraid that anything I say will send her back down the hole. Besides, what do you talk about with someone who doesn't leave the house? I take my wine glass and refill it. My mother either doesn't notice or doesn't care. I squat over the box of ornaments and start looking through them.

"We have to do the lights first." She pulls me over, and we start the wrapping process. When we're done, the tree looks like a dark valley filled with tiny red, green, and gold stars you want to run through.

"Can I hang ornaments now?" I ask, feeling nostalgic. My mom gives me a nod and refills her glass. I find the glue-covered-macaroni-elementary-school-picture-of-Mya-wear-ing-braces ornament and laugh. She used to hide this one every year. I pull out my stocking and stuff it in there.

"Don't do them all without me." My mom wiggles her body next to me and starts rummaging through the tiny glass bulbs and hand-sewn Santa Clauses. I look for my favorites and scatter them around the tree.

"What else has been going on?" She asks after a few moments of silence.

"I'm probably the worst person to ask. I'm almost as anti-social as you are." I take another sip of wine.

"So I'm supposed to believe that you've just been talking to yourself up in your room?" I focus on the tree and reach my hand into its center, feeling it's trunk. I didn't expect my mom to actually be listening.

"What else do you hear?"

"Just you. Coming in at night, taking a shower, cleaning." Why does existence have to be so noisy?

"I'm glad you've been conscious for some of the last few months," I say. I think of my mom lying in her bed in the dark, listening to me and my footsteps trailing throughout the house, how lonely that must've felt. I touch the back of her shoulder, and she stops moving. I wrap my arms around her middle and rest my head against her back. But it's a comfort I wanted given, not taken. The feeling isn't as satisfying as I hoped it to be. I release my grasp and back away. My mom turns around and squeezes my arm. She sits down on the couch.

"It looks beautiful," she says. I nod, agreeing with her. "It reminds me of one of your father's office Christmas parties. There was a huge tree in the front corner of the office, like this one, with presents all around it. This happened a while ago, and back then people got wasted at these parties. There was always a full bar, and everyone drank." She takes the last sip from her glass, and I refill it.

"Thank you," she says and pats my hand. "One of your father's co-workers, who was fairly new to the company and pretty young, had way too much and couldn't handle his liquor. About halfway through the night, he bends down and vomits all over the presents. I saw the whole thing happen, as if in slow motion, and almost puked myself." I chuckle, remembering my mom's sense of humor. "Your father tried to cover my eyes, but it was too late."

"I'm glad our Christmas tree reminds you of puke smeared gifts." I look over at my mom, and she smiles at me. I love Christmas.

CHAPTER 13

It SNOWS a few times leading up to Christmas. The roads back up enough to make my commute to work a few minutes longer. The only inconvenience this causes is to my poor fingers, which are numb by the time I walk into Price's. The heat in my mom's car isn't working, and I don't have the time or energy to fix it.

"Good evening, Autumn," Kelvin says, smiling from ear to ear underneath a red Santa hat. I cup my hands together and breathe into them. The holidays have put everyone in a good mood. I even heard Greg laugh last week while talking to a customer. The store's been busier than usual as people rush in to get last minute wrapping paper and cheap toys for distant relatives.

"How's it going, Kelvin?" I ask after hanging my coat in the back next to Greg's office. There's a line, so I don't expect him to answer me. Instead I jump on the next register and start ringing up items. It's nice sharing almost an entire shift with someone. Kelvin brings the store to life. He's so cheery, everyone can't help but leave smiling. It slows down around dinner time, and we spend some time tidying up and re-stocking.

"Any holiday plans?" I ask, interrupting his whistling rendition of some corny Christmas song.

"Not really. I'm just going to hang out with my dad and brother and then visit the grandparents. They live a little further upstate, but my grandma makes the best apple pie you could eat." Kelvin licks his lips. "What about you?"

"I'll probably just end up watching some cheesy holiday movie." I think of the tree in our living room and smile. Mya used to love watching Hallmark Christmas movies. She'd force me to sit with her on Christmas Eve as we sucked on candy canes until our mouths were dry, our legs restless. If my mom chooses to join me, tomorrow may even feel sort of normal.

"Before I leave, I got you something," Kelvin blurts out. I look at the clock and notice it's almost time for him to go, which means only one more hour of my shift. Kelvin disappears in the back and comes out with a wrapped box. "It's just something small," he says while putting on his coat. I didn't expect him to get me anything, and I feel guilty for not being as considerate. To be honest, I completely forgot about the present aspect of Christmas. It's not like I'm expecting to get anything this year. Holding the present in my hands I suddenly feel like crying. Kelvin goes up to the register and starts counting out his drawer. I take a deep breath as he continues to whistle Christmas songs. My fingers tremble as I undo the packaging and pull out a pair of black winter gloves. I look up at Kelvin and notice him smiling at me.

"Thank you," I mouth, and he nods his head.

"Merry Christmas, Autumn." His whistling is stuck in my head for the rest of my shift. A couple more customers come in, and I keep the shop open for a few extra minutes in case there's any stragglers. Greg comes in right before I'm about to lock the door.

"I just have to cash out my drawer," I tell him, walking back to the register.

"How did today go?" He asks and leans against the counter.

"We were pretty busy," I say, handing him Kelvin's bank bag. He opens it and smiles at all the green. I write out the numbers in my drawer on receipt paper and hand the slip to Greg.

"The holidays will carry us a few more months," Greg says, but I think it's directed more to himself than me. "Merry Christmas, Autumn." Greg disappears into his back office, and I lock the front doors. Before I walk to my car I put on the black gloves. The drive home is significantly more enjoyable, and I silently thank Kelvin the entire way.

The house is quiet when I walk in, and I let it stay that way. I go right up to my room and lay down. The inside of my body feels heavy and my mind is wired. I think of Kelvin and his cheery Christmas spirit. I've been so busy with work, school, and May that I haven't painted in a while. I stand up and sift through the canvases leaning against my bedroom wall, pulling out one featuring a woman looking out of a window. It's something I made over a year ago. I remember how excited I was when I finished it. It was one of my first times exploring with water colors, and I had a difficult time getting the shading right. It looks simple and empty now.

I place the painting on my desk and outline the woman's face with a black pen so that it stands out. I want to add something next to her, but I don't have any water color paint left. Instead I sneak into the kitchen and gather all of the nature and entertainment magazines we've received in the past few months. I rip out pages and cut out images with the tip of a box cutter. I haven't made a collage since my freshman year art class, and I just now remember how much I enjoyed doing it. I work on the painting until my body is too exhausted to keep going. I sleep for a few hours until the sound of Christmas music wakes me up.

I take a quick shower and walk downstairs to find my mom sitting on the couch looking at a set of Polaroid pictures. I pause for a moment, looking at the bookshelf where the family photo album hides behind.

"You don't remember, but this is your first Christmas," my mom says, holding out a picture. I hesitate before sitting down. "You hardly slept that night. Between Mya's excitement and your crying, it was the most exhausting Christmas morning your father and I ever had." She laughs.

"God, what am I wearing?" I gasp at the hideous dress, frills and floral covering my 6-month old body.

"I picked those out," My mom exclaims, and I notice that Mya wears a matching one in another photo. It's not like I have any sense of fashion, so I let my mother's dress choice go without harassing her. I sort through the pictures and find one of my parents, a lot younger, sitting in front of a mantel with stockings hung behind them. They look like kids, but they did meet when they were young—college, I think. I look at my mom, afraid that she'll have a negative reaction, but she seems happy.

"Do you want tea?" I ask, standing up. The pictures make my heart sink and my head feel dizzy. They're from a life I don't even know, a life I can't relate to, but I guess I'm glad my mother enjoys the nostalgia.

"I already made some." She points to the kettle, and I pour some hot water in a mug. It's sunny outside, and I realize it's later in the morning than I previously thought. "There's some eggs in the pan as well," my mom says, but the words sound unsure, like she's self-conscious of making breakfast. I try to act like it's all normal and pull out a plate. She sits at the kitchen table and watches me eat.

"You probably don't remember, but when you were a toddler someone from your father's work gave you and Mya these glass dolls," my mom begins but stops to take a sip of tea. "We didn't know what they were before you guys unwrapped them. In fact, I think we forgot about them, and Mya found them behind the tree later that day. Anyway, she pulled out the boxes and gave one to you. You loved opening presents. What kid doesn't?" She smiles and waves her hand in the air.

"You probably dropped the box a dozen times though before you successfully opened it, and by the time we could see what it was, the doll was in pieces. We had to throw it out, but you didn't really care. To be honest, you never really played with dolls, but Mya felt so bad for you. She gave you her doll, which you immediately dropped on the floor and then stepped all over. Mya was traumatized. Your feet were covered in blood."

Hearing this story kills my appetite for some reason. I try to shake it off, but my hands won't stop trembling. My mind tries to sort out if this is normal or not, if I should engage my mother in childhood tales of her dead daughter. But the story paces through me like venom, and I want to feel Mya's tears dripping down my cheek. I want to hear my father's voice filled with panic, and I also want to push all of those feelings down and pretend that none of it ever happened. The island was lonely, but I had control. I could pick what thoughts I engaged in.

"Are you okay?" I hear my mom ask. I realize my breathing is heavy.

"I think I need some fresh air," I tell her and stand up. She stands up too and walks me to the door.

"Come back soon," she says and smiles. I can tell she doesn't want me to go, and I have to choke down a thick gum of guilt before opening the door and sprinting into the cold air. I keep my eyes focused ahead of me and resist the urge to turn around.

I walk the few blocks to May's house and knock on the front door. May answers and immediately throws her arms around me. "Merry Christmas, Autumn," she whispers into my ear. I pull away and kiss her even though my lips are numb.

"I was just about to come and get you," she says, pulling me into the house.

"For what?" The house is a bit cold, and it's emptier than I thought it'd be on Christmas Eve. May leads me upstairs and stops in front of a room I've never been in before.

"Your Christmas present." She pulls out a grocery bag and hands me a pair of lab goggles.

"Thanks?" I hold the goggles up, confused.

"You have to put these on too." She pulls out a black-hooded sweatshirt and matching sweatpants.

"Are we robbing a convenience store?" I ask, putting the sweatshirt on anyway.

"No, this is just for safety purposes." She opens the door and holds her arm out, signaling me to walk inside. I step in slowly, greeted with what looks like the inside of a junk shop.

"May, what is this?" I tap a three-legged chair with the tip of my boot and it falls over with a 'thunk.'

"I thought you needed a way to get out some of your anger, and I didn't think I could convince you to join a sports team. This seemed like the next best thing." She smiles and hands me a bat.

"What are we doing?" I watch as May slowly brings her bat into the air behind her head.

"Destroying everything." She smiles, then slams the bat down. Glass shatters everywhere. The noise startles me.

"Are you sure this is okay?" I look around the room at all the glass plates and cheap furniture.

"I've been collecting this stuff for weeks now. Most of it was dumped on the side of the road. I also went to a few flea markets for the tables." She nudges a rickety nightstand, and the lamp on top of it shakes. "Swing away."

I've never considered myself a violent person, but the act of demolishing every day, ordinary objects seems innocently therapeutic. I lift the bat over my shoulder and ram it into a light blue oriental looking lamp. It fills the floor with a wiry ocean. I watch the glass sparkle in the dim lighting of the room and smile at May. We go crazy. I hit through tables, broken chairs, and plates. Glass and splinters of wood fly through the air. I beat an old TV to pieces. My voice breaks through the air as I yell. I swing the bat harder and faster, my skin starting to sweat. I yell my fucking lungs out.

It feels like time has slowed as we carry on with our destruction. Eventually, the room is full of rubble. I drop the bat on the floor, my body feeling worn, drained.

"I hope you brought garbage bags," I say, wincing. My voice is sore and raspy.

"I'll take care of cleanup tomorrow. Let's go rest. I'm winded." May leans on her bat, panting slightly. I nod, and we leave the room. I take off the protective attire and lay down on her bed. She sits next to me and plays with my hair.

"You should be a therapist, you've helped me so much." I stretch and move my head onto May's lap. I feel her stomach flex as she chuckles.

"I think my methods might be a bit unorthodox." She

cups my cheek and smiles down at me. I yawn and nuzzle closer to her.

"Autumn, I think this method of expression helps, but it's only a temporary solution. You should direct that emotion into something more."

"Something more...?" I trail off. My eyelids start to feel heavy, and I let them rest.

"Just something with meaning. Use it as fuel to help." I feel her fingers trace my brow.

"Good idea," I mumble. I can hear May talking, but the sound grows further away, and my head feels like it's slowly sinking into dreams.

I wake up suddenly and immediately sit upright. I see that the sky's already dark and run out of May's room. There wasn't supposed to be a sleepover tonight. Hopefully my mom hasn't noticed. That's pretty unlikely though.

I run home as fast as I can. I have no idea what time it is. Damn. Hopefully it's not already Christmas. I open the front door inch by inch, attempting to be quiet. The living room light is on, and my mom is sitting on the couch. She stands up as soon as she sees me. I wait for her to yell or say something. She opens her arms and takes half a step forward but then stops.

"I was worried about you," she says, her voice slightly above a whisper. I stand in the doorway for a moment, looking at her. I immediately want to say something bitter, but the thought of her waiting for me to come home all night, not knowing where I am, with one daughter already in the grave, drives in my guilt.

"I'm sorry," I say, looking down at my feet. She sits back down, and I hear her pat the cushion next to her.

"Come here. I've made some tea." I close the door and pour myself a glass before joining her on the couch. The tree is lit up in front of us, and it actually feels a little nice, even though there aren't any presents underneath it. "So, is there a boyfriend?" she asks after a moment of silence.

"No, I was just at a friend's house and accidently fell asleep." I watch my mother nod her head slowly.

"It's okay if you're having sex, Autumn. I'd just like to talk to you about it." Hearing my mom say the word 'sex' is like sniffing spoiled milk.

"I'm not." I feel my face redden and take a sip of tea. My mom lets it go and walks away. I lean back against the couch, feeling exhausted and awake at the same time.

"I know this isn't a normal present, but I thought you'd appreciate it more than a gift." She comes back and hands me a folded piece of paper. I reach for it, and her arm pulls away slightly, as if she's unsure, but then she quickly hands it to me. It's an appointment slip for therapy. My mother's eyes remain fixed on the floor, but I stare up at her.

"Why now?" I ask, clutching the paper.

"I just feel ready I guess," she says, her voice hardly above a whisper. She doesn't look at me, and I notice the slight quiver of her bottom lip.

"There's nothing wrong with needing help." I set the paper down and touch her arm. Her lips, her whole body is trembling. "Mom, it's going to be okay." I brush the hair out of her face, and she touches my hand.

"I'm sorry," she says, her voice cracking. I didn't know how badly I wanted to hear those words until after they leave her mouth. Tears trickle down my cheeks, but I smile and nod. My mother wraps her arms around me, and I rest into her, feeling safe again.

CHAPTER 14

LATE WINTER LEAVES me longing for spring, although I don't mind the quietness it's entranced upon our town. Price's is back to its usual dusty-shelved pace, so I cut back on shifts and spend more time at home or with May. At night, I lay awake and think about the world and all the details that make it feel so complicated. Sometimes I try to draw this, but it's just too big to encumber, or maybe I'm thinking too small. Either way, the days and nights seem to merge, and when I brush my fingers across the wood panels on my bedroom floor they feel full, like I could sink my teeth into the timber and suck water from its splinters.

My mom leaves the house twice a week for a little over an hour. When it snows she goes outside and shovels, and I stand in the kitchen and watch her. She usually lasts about 30 minutes and then comes inside where we switch roles. Except when I come back inside, she's sitting on the couch with a glass of wine.

"What? I'm recovering. I can guiltlessly sip on some red." She'd always liked to drink, and when she did, it was like we were on an exciting venture where everything was funny. To be honest, I give her props for it not becoming a problem when shit hit the fan.

"These eyes aren't judging you for *that*. You shoveled way less than half," I say, pointing at the driveway.

"You're young. You're capable of doing more than me and my old back," she says, waving me over to the couch. The wine bottle and another glass are on the coffee table. "This is the bottle of wine your dad got me on our 10th wedding anniversary." She pours a little in the second glass and hands it to me. Occasionally, she'll want me to taste one of the bottles she's opened, but I don't have the pallet for wine yet. I take a sip of the dark liquid and manage to swallow it without my face twisting in disgust.

"This one actually isn't so bad," I tell her and walk to the kitchen for a cup of water. "Why are you opening that one now?" I ask between sips.

"I'm revisiting the good times." It's something I know she discussed in therapy, and I'm glad it's making her happy, but it's hard for me to see it laid out in the open so simply.

"What did you and Dad do on your first dates?" I lean back into the couch and put my feet on the coffee table.

"We liked to go on picnics." My mom nods and smiles. "We'd sit in the grass, sipping wine and eating bread smeared with cheese, watching the sparrows fly overhead." My mom shudders slightly. "I can still feel the breeze," she says, her voice so soft I can hardly make out the words. Her eyes fixate on the carpet in front of her, and I can tell that she isn't sitting next to me but is seasons away, a blue sky over her head.

"In a few months you'll be able to have days like that again," I tell her, trying to sound positive in the hope that maybe she'll start leaving the house on a daily basis. She's definitely more active, but every time I come home and see her sitting on the couch, a heaviness falls in my chest that sucks the air out of my lungs.

"Yeah, that'd be nice. We'll have to go out of town for the wine." She scuffs.

"You don't have to drink every bottle in Dad's collection before then," I say, giving her a hard time.

"It was *our* collection, not just his," my mom boasts and takes another sip from her glass. I remember my dad pulling together lavish, romantic dinners in our dining room when Mya was too sick for us to go out to a restaurant together. He loved to cook. He'd spend hours in the kitchen, patiently waiting and working to create gourmet dinners. That passion died when dinners were mostly spent separated and purchased for three dollars from a menu. Though on some occasions, when Mya was home and the tension wasn't sticking to us like a shadow, my dad would set the table and bring out a dish he cooked my mom in their early years of marriage. She'd actually smile on those nights, and it looked genuine.

"I bet there'll be a snow day tomorrow," I say, looking out the window. My mom closes her eyes slightly and nods her head.

"At best you'll get a delay. The snow's stopping soon, and it'll be warmer weather the rest of the week. Everything's going to melt."

"Cheers to that." I clink my water cup against the rim of her wine glass.

The urge to daydream during my classes grows stronger as the afternoons seem to widen. In Mr. Busman's Economics class, I struggle to pay attention, but his loud voice this morning keeps everyone awake.

"An oligopoly is a market in which a few large firms dominate a market. Can anyone give an example?" He calls out. I look at May resting her chin against her hand, gently twirling her hair.

"Autumn, an example?" I look forward and immediately feel my face burn.

"Of what?" I ask, startled. Everyone else in the class seems half asleep, so I try to relax a bit.

"An oligopoly." He waits a few minutes as I rack my brain.

"The Super Center?" I ask, thinking of all the business it's taken away from our small town.

"Good, Autumn." Mr. Busman is about to continue, but a girl in the first row raises her hand.

"Isn't the Super Center a monopoly since it dominates the market?" she asks. Mr. Busman actually smiles and nods his head.

"Well, if you look at the Super Center in the perspective of a small family business then the answer could be yes. The Super Center is so big that it drives smaller businesses out of business, so it does dominate the market in that respect. However, the Super Center isn't the 'single seller' of many of its items."

"So it's a perfect competition?" The same girl asks, but this time her tone is pitched in a way that challenges Mr. Busman's authority. Without thinking I raise my hand.

"Yes, Autumn." Mr. Busman calls on me, and this time many eyes turn around to stare at my hand slowly drawing down.

"I'm just wondering, what can a small business do to compete with the Super Center?" My voice is quiet, but I think of Price's—Greg, Kelvin, and the slow hours.

"I don't know, but maybe focusing on something that the

larger firm doesn't have to offer could help." Mr. Busman pauses a moment, and I lean back in my chair. He continues talking, but I catch May looking back at me. I offer her a small smile and bend over my notebook.

I start writing a list of all the services and products that the Super Center doesn't offer. I have to keep going back and crossing off lines as there are already so many items the Super Center sells. Then I have to go back and cross off items that another small business in our town already focuses on. I continue the list throughout the day, and by the end I only have a handful ideas that seem helpful.

"Fancy a drive before you have to start your shift?" May asks, wrapping her arms around my middle.

"Of course." I hold her hand, and we walk through the parking lot in silence. The clouds move quickly overhead, and I think it might storm later. A good spring shower would be nice. I unlock the doors, and we start on our usual back road route in the outskirts of town.

"Is something on your mind, darling?" May asks after a few moments. Her fingers trace behind my ear, and I exhale.

"Sorry, I know I'm quiet." I give her a quick side-ways smile.

"That's nothing to apologize for. I'm just wondering what you're thinking about." Her hand moves down my shoulder so that she's gently rubbing the back of my neck. I pull over on a side street and put the car in park.

"I've spent all day trying to think of a way Price's can stay in business. I've come up with a list, but all my ideas are shit, and I don't know if I should even broach the subject with Greg because what do I know? I don't even have plans for my own future, let alone a business." I take a deep breath and realize that I'm actually nervous. My stomach does a leap, and I grip the steering wheel.

"Hey." May cups her hand over mine. "It's okay. No one's expecting you to solve this problem." Her words are smooth and manage to calm me.

"I know," I start to say, but May cuts me off.

"You're also a lot smarter than you give yourself credit for." She points her finger in my direction and tilts her head to look up at me. I manage a small smile.

"I guess I just care about them, Kelvin and Greg, and I want everything to be okay," I say, realizing my emotional pull for the first time. It stuns me; I can't remember the last time I cared about anyone else outside of my family and May. The feeling leaves me bothered and exposed.

"I'm so selfish," I exclaim, staring straight ahead, wide-eyed. May laughs.

"Are you crazy? You're talking about trying to help your friends."

"I haven't been a good friend, May." I look down into my lap. May nudges me to look up at her.

"That's okay, darling. Everyone understands that you've been going through a rough patch, and besides, there's time to make up for any shortcomings." She leans in and kisses me softly. The warmth elevates my spirits, and I nod my head.

"You're so amazing," I say, and kiss her as if I'm trying to stamp a piece of myself on her skin. We drive back into town, and I drop May off before making my way to Price's. I put my scribbled up list into my pocket and enter the store. Kelvin is leaning against the counter and jumps as the door slams shut.

"Hey Autumn," he stutters. "How's it going?" The store is empty, and Greg isn't in his back office.

"Can I talk to you about something before I bring it up to Greg?" I ask, stepping behind the counter. I only have about an hour with Kelvin before his shift ends, and I want to ask him if any of these ideas are plausible.

"Yeah, are you okay?" Kelvin asks, sitting up straight. I take out my list and open it on the counter, spreading my hand over the creases so that it's laid out straight.

"I've been thinking all day about how Price's could survive, and one of the options the store has is focusing on items that the Super Center doesn't sell," I say in one breath.

"Theory of evolution, we adapt to survive?" Kelvin asks, and I nod my head. "But the Super Center sells everything."

"I made a list, and I know it's not a lot of options, but maybe we could brainstorm a bit together and propose the idea to Greg?" I wipe my palms on my jeans and try to stop twisting my fingers.

"I think you already have the winning idea here." Kelvin points to the line scribbled 'wine shop'. It was inspired by my mother, but I think it might be difficult to completely change the store in such a way. "Although, there's probably special permits or regulations we'd have to abide by. I think you're right though. This shop is way too general, and shifting to a more specialized market could be more profitable." I watch Kelvin, how his shoulders sag, and his mouth closes tightly.

"What's wrong?" He looks defeated.

"Autumn, I brought up the idea of shifting gears with Greg a few months ago. The conversation went fine, but I guess it didn't fly over well when he discussed it with his father."

"Why?" Greg's dad has to understand that it's not Greg's fault the store is losing customers to the competition.

"Why change something that's working fine?" Kelvin asks, and I raise my eyebrows in question. "I think Greg's been lying about our profits. He must've taken out a loan or something."

"How can his father believe that?" I'm shocked. Greg must be buried in debt at this point.

"Customer loyalty?" Kelvin shrugs. "I don't know, but it won't go well when everything comes out."

"You should talk to him, Kelvin. His father wouldn't want this if he knew," I say, shaking my head.

"Probably not." Kelvin pauses and runs his fingers through his dark hair, which glistens in the overhead light. "But you should talk to him. I've already breached the conversation, and besides, it might help to hear this from someone else." Kelvin looks sideways at me, and I nod my head slowly. I understand where he's coming from, but Greg and I don't really chat. Our conversations have always been focused on my work and the store, but I guess this relates.

"If he didn't listen to you, I don't think he'll listen to me," I mumble.

"Whether he listens or not isn't really the point. I mean, this situation is beyond either of our control. Ultimately Greg will do what he wants, but his decisions affect us, and I think that's worth something." He has a point.

The rest of my shift ticks by slowly after Kelvin leaves. A handful of customers come in before the sky starts to darken, and then I focus on cleaning up. I know every inch of this shop, and I long ago memorized where every item sits on its shelves. The thought of everything changing ties an anchor around my heart, but the inevitable lifts my sail. If I'm going to try and influence those changes then I have to talk to Greg. I wait around a few extra minutes until Greg shuffles through the door. He mumbles a greeting and begins to walk back to his office.

"Hey," I call after him and he turns. "I wanted to ask you something." He pauses in front of the counter and faces me.

"Is something wrong?" The rings around his eyes are as

deep as a bathtub drain, and there's a subtle smell of dried sweat.

"I know what it feels like to not want to disappoint someone." It isn't what I planned on saying, but the words leave my mouth before I have time to consider the consequences. Greg shifts his shoulders back and his fingers slowly clench together. "And I know how it feels to be stuck in a relentless loop with no clear window to daylight," I say in one quick breath. "Greg, there are options here. Price's doesn't have to dig a grave yet, not like this. You care about this town, and so do I." I don't expect the words to ring true as they leave my mouth, but they settle into me with a warm glow.

"Greg, you can fix this." I pause, and Greg looks down at the counter. "You're not alone. Kelvin and I, we want to help."

Greg takes a deep breath and rubs the back of his neck.

"What do you propose?" he asks with a small smile.

CHAPTER 15

NOTHING CHANGES after my conversation with Greg. He politely listened to me and said that he'd discuss the possibility of restructuring the shop with his dad. A few weeks have gone by though, and nothing's happened. I don't take it personally, but I'm nervous for him, and the situation has put a space in our relationship. It's like he's afraid to speak to me lest I confront him about the inevitable.

I spend time with May, walking in the woods behind her house. The snow is almost gone, and the weather is warm in the afternoons. We climb trees together, like children, and hide above the world. I collect stones and line them on the sill of my window. At night, when my head is resting in the nook of May's arm, I try to make out the rocks in the moonlight. I spend hours counting them and watching the light glisten off their smooth surfaces.

"Are you sleeping?" I whisper into the darkness. I put my hand on May's chest and feel it rise and fall in rhythm to her breathing.

"Yes," she murmurs. She turns on her side, and I follow suit in front of her so that she's holding me. I wiggle myself as tight as I can against her and play with her fingers extended from the arm wrapped around me.

"Are you afraid to die?" I ask. The room remains silent. "It's crazy to think about. Your existence, everything that's ever happened to you—your story—gone, dissolved off the face of the earth as soon as you stop breathing." I exhale, leaning even further into May. "And we all go about our days not paying that fact any mind, like the thought doesn't warrant crippling anxiety." May pulls me tight and nuzzles her head into the back of my shoulders. I feel her lips kiss behind my neck.

"We all have some sort of history we leave behind, darling. And there's little control any of us have over death, so why spend life in a constant state of worry and panic?" She brushes my hair back and leans forward to kiss me on the cheek. The gesture makes me smile, and my head falls deeper into my pillow.

All of my classes become either lackadaisical or chaotic. We're so close to graduating that at this point our teachers are just as excited to see us off as we are to leave. I watch my peers form into little cliques of chit chat towards the end of every class. I sometimes follow conversations or just zone out. A few of my old friends smile at me as they talk, but besides that I could be invisible. After English class Ms. Rogan idles at my desk while everyone walks out.

"Hi Autumn," she says, smiling. I stop packing and look up at her. "Have any plans this summer?"

"Just working." I shrug. She nods while twisting her fingers.

"How are you doing?" She looks me in the eyes, and I can

make out the start of crow's feet imprinted behind the corners of her glasses.

"I'm fine," I say out of instinct. "Just excited to finally graduate." I flash a smile.

"Do you have plans yet for the fall?"

"You mean, have I picked a college and major to commit the rest of my life to?" I raise my eyebrows, and she chuckles.

"It's a ridiculous thing to ask of an 18-year-old, I know. However, you can study something general and leave yourself open for more job options. And you can change majors if you don't like what you're studying." She sits down at the desk next to me. "There are so many possibilities." We look at each other, and she rolls her eyes. "I sound like Mrs. Nelson, don't I?" The comment makes me laugh.

"You're not that bad," I tease.

"Listen, I know that you're going to figure everything out, but Mrs. Nelson told me today that you're one of the only students who doesn't have a plan once they graduate, so I just wanted to make sure you've talked about your options."

"I appreciate that, and if I have any questions I'll come to you." I stand up, and Ms. Rogan opens her mouth as if she wants to say more but just nods. I can't help but feel like a bug under a microscope when teachers corner me.

After school May finds me in the parking lot to go for a drive before I have to work. We listen to music, and May plays with my hair as she looks out the window. At the red lights, I trace her jaw line, brushing my fingers over her tanned skin.

"What are you thinking about?" She asks me.

"What I'm going to do with the rest of my life," I answer slowly.

"What have you come up with so far?" Her hand moves down to my forearm, and I feel a gentle squeeze.

"What constitutes a plan? Does a general idea suffice, or should I submit a formal outline to some corporate mailbox?" I exhale out of my nose.

"I'm not one to judge," May whispers. "There must be something you're interested in though."

"I want to help people." I feel the tip of May's fingers gently brush against my cheek as she pushes hair behind my ear.

"I think that's a great start," she encourages.

"How though? There's so much that needs to be done."

"That's for you to figure out, darling," she says while kissing up my neck. I focus on the road, and her lips leave me wanting more. I push the feeling away and drop May off at her house.

"I'm excited for you," she says as she jumps out of the car. I give her a puzzled look as she turns around. "There are so many possibilities ahead." She kisses me quick and waves me off.

At work Kelvin and I play tic-tac-toe on receipt paper. Now that the weather is warmer more pedestrians are out walking. This doesn't really mean there's an influx of customers, just that we can do more people watching.

"I can't wait for summer," Kelvin exclaims. "I need a break from class."

"When do you finish?" I ask, drawing a line through three X's.

"Semester ends in a few weeks." Kelvin draws a new grid and places an 'O' in a slot.

"I mean, when are you finished with school altogether?"

"I don't know." Kelvin pauses and contemplates his next move. "I'll eventually have to transfer to a four-year school to get my bachelor's, but not until I have a more defined idea of what I want to do." I scribble out the game and set my pen down. "I was going to win that one."

"It was going to be a tie." I clench my fingers into my palm. "So we're in the same boat. I have no idea what I'm doing either."

"You sound distressed." Kelvin leans forward into the counter and looks up at me.

"It's a bit distressing." I raise my eyebrows, expecting him to agree.

"It shouldn't be," he says. "You get to explore all these new topics. Topics that will excite you because you'll have an interest in what you're learning. College isn't like high school. I took a class last semester where we watched a movie twice a week and then wrote a reflection paper."

"You make it sound fantastical." I try to imagine myself on a college campus where no one knows me, where I'm a stranger. It'd be a chance to start my life over. Could I really leave? My mom's doing better. She doesn't need me. I push the thoughts away and draw on receipt paper until my shift ends.

When I open the front door there's two mugs on the kitchen table, and the kettle is heating. My mom stands by the sink with a sponge in her hand. There's a lit candle on the counter top. It feels like home. I smile to myself and breathe in the warmth.

"Are you hungry?" she asks, drying her hands on a dish rag.

"No, but tea would be lovely." I sit down at the table, and my mom brings over the kettle.

"How was school?" She sits across from me and tosses

me a tea bag. I dip it into my mug repeatedly and think of Ms. Rogan's conversation about my future.

"I'm glad it's almost done." I lean forward and blow into the steaming liquid.

"It feels like yesterday you started kindergarten." My mom looks down and smiles. I imagine her remembering my first day of school, how I looked back at her when stepping onto the bus, not wanting to leave. I have a faint memory of the anxiety I felt in that moment.

"How was your day?" The steam warms my face as I try to take a small sip without burning myself.

"Fine." She pauses for a moment to blow on her tea. "I had a good therapy session." Her voice shakes. I try to offer an encouraging nod.

"What did you talk about?" I'm curious about what my mother says during her sessions. I wonder how she depicts me, but that's assuming she mentions me at all.

"I have so many awful memories, from the past few years of Mya being sick, from my childhood," she says, the last part softly. "They play on a loop in my mind, daily. It's hard to see past it. When I woke up this morning, I thought back to when your father made me breakfast in bed on Sunday mornings when we first started dating. We'd read the paper together and work on the puzzles until noon." She takes another sip of tea, and I wait for her to continue.

"It's so much easier to remember the negative memories. The pain. The shit that happened every damn day." She pauses for a moment and shakes her head. "I forgot what it was like to just sit in the sun, the clouds, or any type of storm and just appreciate." She keeps her eyes locked on the kitchen table as she takes a sip of tea.

"There's too much I've been taking for granted." She looks me in the eyes, and I look away. Whatever she's trying to do right now, whatever she's trying to give, I don't want it. My lips twitch into a smile, and I make a noise in my throat that resembles a laugh. Her eyebrows tug together, and her mouth gapes open as if a question hangs off her tongue, but she doesn't say anything. I nod my head and stand up, walking backwards until I reach the hallway and then turn around and run into my bedroom. I close the door and slide to the floor, pressing my shoulders into the wood. I inhale as much air as I can in one breath. There's something in my chest, something screaming inside of me, but I push it down.

What is wrong with me? I should be happy that my mom is finally recovering, but instead a bitterness grows inside of me, something that feels even worse than anger. My hands shake, and I clench them into fists and hold them tightly in front of my mouth. I focus on breathing and close my eyes. There's a soft knock on the door that vibrates behind my head.

"Autumn," I hear through the wood in a whispered voice. "Are you okay?" I bite into my knuckle and wrestle the bone between my teeth.

"It's not enough," I choke into my skin. She doesn't move, and I imagine her hand and her cheek pressed on the other side of the door as she tries to listen for my presence. I imagine myself falling into the timber and landing in her lap. It makes the screaming louder.

"It's not enough," I repeat and turn so that my cheek rests on the door too. I hold my hand to my chest with a feeling of wanting more. Is that what fuels this rage inside of me? I soften my voice and kneel, facing the door. "I'm okay, mom. I'm just tired."

She doesn't walk away immediately. Her feet leave shadows that dance in hesitation under the slit of the door. I want to stick my fingers through and touch her. I also want to pound the wood until I break through and then grab her.

"I'm going to bed." My voice feels horse, but I try to elevate it so that I know she hears me. I listen as she shuffles around and slowly walks down the stairs, one step at a time. I sit back down, hug my knees to my chest, and close my eyes until the day's events don't matter.

CHAPTER 16

I WAKE up to the doorbell, an extremely rare noise. I quickly throw on an old t-shirt and sweatpants and rush downstairs. Before opening the door, I peer through the window curtain and notice a mess of short, black, greasy hair.

"Kelvin?" I open the door and stare at him in confusion. He looks down at me and smiles.

"Hi Autumn. I'm glad I got the number right," he says, eyeing the front of my house up and down.

"How did you?"

"It was listed on your application at Price's. I found it in a pile under the counter." He smiles.

"Does that mean you cleaned and organized this morning?" I glance behind me at the clock and notice that Kelvin should be working his shift. A rush of concern causes my stomach to flip. "Is everything okay?" I open the door wider and Kelvin takes a step forward.

"Yeah, I just wanted to talk to you. Is it okay if I come in?" I nod my head and close the door behind him. We sit at the kitchen table, and I peep over at my mother's closed bedroom door. She's such a heavy sleeper.

"Do you want anything to drink?" I ask, standing to put the kettle on.

"Coffee or tea would be great if you're making some." I nod and watch out of the corner of my eye as he cautiously takes in my living situation.

"So, what do I owe this visit?" I sit back down as the water heats. Kelvin sighs and leans forward so that his elbows rest on the table.

"Well, I have some news about Price's. Greg told me this morning, but I wanted to be the one to give you the update." He pauses, and I inch my chair closer. "Greg talked to his dad." I can't help but gape as I feel my eyes widen.

"How did it go?" I ask. Kelvin leans back and runs a hand through his hair, causing pieces of dried skin to fall onto his shoulders.

"Well, he agrees that Price's needs to be restructured. I guess he liked the wine store idea, but they have to look into that being a possibility." I can't help but smile.

"That's good, right?" I ask and stand to pour the tea. Kelvin watches me as I pull out two mugs. His silence causes me to turn around.

"Overall, yes." I hand Kelvin the mug and sit back down.

"What's the catch?" I ask matter-of-factly. Kelvin offers a slight smile.

"When Greg's dad found out how the store's really doing, he demanded Greg close down immediately." He wraps his hand around the mug and looks down into the cup. "We aren't employed anymore."

"Oh." I lean back into my chair. "No offense Kelvin, but why are you delivering this news? Isn't it Greg's responsibility?" It's a lot to process, and I take a sip of my tea to stop from asking more questions.

"He wanted to. He told me this morning when I came in.

He was going to call you, but I told him I wanted to be the one to tell you." He takes his time saying the words, looking just past me.

"I guess a personalized visit is nice." I smirk. "Is there a reason why you wanted to tell me though?" Kelvin shifts in his seat.

"I knew that I wouldn't see you again aside from just around town here or there if Greg gave you a phone call. I figured this way I could at least say goodbye and thank you for all the help." Kelvin pauses to take a sip of tea. "Greg was a fine boss, but he didn't see everything you did for Price's." He looks into my eyes, and I notice the emotion stirring inside of him. I try to act at ease, but I'm not used to such blatant exposure.

"Thank you, Kelvin. That means a lot." I reach out and squeeze his hand, trying not to think of how unclean it probably is. We sit in silence for a moment, drinking tea and listening to the birds outside.

"What will you do?" I ask him after a moment. Kelvin shrugs.

"I don't have it figured out yet. Greg said he'd hire me back if he opened up again. I think in the meantime I'll spend time with my family and work on some side projects. I'll look for odd jobs this summer and see if there's any openings elsewhere." I take in a deep breath and exhale.

"You sound calm about it," I say and tuck my feet underneath the chair, trying to bring myself together. The anxiety of losing my job causes my hands to shake. I have some money in savings, but the thought of not having an income leaves me feeling less than secure.

"I guess we knew this would happen eventually." Kelvin reaches into his pocket and pulls out a white envelope. He puts it on the table in front of me. "This is from Greg." I stare at it and then at him. "It's your last pay check. Well, it's cash, not a check."

I pick up the envelope and run my thumb over my name handwritten on the front. I don't want to open it in front of Kelvin, but I'm anxious to do something with my hands. I pick the seal loose and run my fingers through the bills.

"This is more than what's owed to me." I hesitate and look up at Kelvin. He smiles. I run through the bills again. "This is more than double what's owed to me." I put the envelope on the table. "Greg must've made a mistake." I shake my head and exhale loudly.

"No, I think I was wrong. Greg did appreciate you. He just has his own way of showing it." I'm baffled, stuck staring at the table. Kelvin laughs, taps the table, stands up, and stretches his arms behind his head. "I hope to see you around, Autumn. But in case I don't, take care of yourself. And try to relax. There's more fun in life than you realize." He reaches his arms out in front of himself, and I realize he wants to give me a hug. The fact that I may not see Kelvin again leaves me with a mixture of emotion. I sink into his hug and try to ignore the slight quiver pulling at my brow.

"Thank you, Kelvin," I say and pull away. "For everything." I smile and open the front door for him to leave. I watch as he walks down the pathway, steps into his car, and waves one last time before driving off.

I sink onto the front steps and let out a long sigh. I wasn't expecting such an eventful morning. Kelvin's visit did soften the blow, and I'm thankful that he took the time to tell me the news in person. It's still hard to believe, and I'm left unsettled. I can't help but feel guilty. Kelvin wasn't just a co-worker to me, but a close friend, and I didn't recognize that enough.

I get ready for the day and head to May's house. I need to

walk through my thoughts and having some company would be helpful. The air is fresh and warmth has settled in. Spring is in full bloom, and I can almost smell summer. I notice a head of red hair bobbing across the street and wave to Jamie. He's sprinting at full speed but stops when he sees me. I cross over and wait for him to catch his breath as he leans forward, resting his hands on his knees.

"Autumn," he exhales. "Enjoying a morning stroll?" Sweat trickles down the side of his face, and I notice the wet marks forming on the sidewalk around him.

"Jeez, Jamie. How any miles did you run?" I take a step back, allowing him more air to breathe. He gives a small laugh.

"About five," he says with a shrug. "Where you headed?" He bends down and lets his arms hang down in a stretch. His pale white skin is now beat red and slightly freckled from the sun.

"I'm just getting a more relaxed form of exercise." I pretend to stretch next to him and bend sideways to touch my toes. "How do you feel about leaving home?" I ask, lifting my ankle into my hand to stretch what could be my quad.

"Excited, nervous, sad, slightly terrified." Jamie laughs and shrugs, but his shoulders are heavy, and I can tell he's being genuine. He tries to play it off as a joke though. "I'm sorry we only catch up while I'm sweating." He wipes his forehead against the sleeve of his shirt, and the splotches of sweat leave a shadow.

"No worries, I'm certainly not my best these days." I give a small laugh as well, but Jamie averts his eyes and turns his body away.

"See you around, Autumn." He waves behind his shoulder. I watch him run off but keep my hands by my side. May only lives a few blocks further.

I knock on her front door and it swings open immediately. May jumps off her porch steps and into my arms. The breeze tramples through our hair, and I inhale the coolness.

"It's good to see you," she whispers in my ear and nuzzles into my neck. I squeeze her once and pull her away so that we're holding hands, side by side.

We walk together silently towards the river. The willows are brown, ready for spring's renewal, and there's a tint of gray over all things time has permitted to grow. Closer to the river, where the dirt turns to sand, May kicks around the water stones, twigs, and bottle caps—a child's treasure chest. She bends down and puts her hand in the water as the current pulls forward. I reach down behind her and pick up one of the bottle caps.

"I used to collect these when I was little." I roll my thumb over the ridges.

"That's disgusting." May laughs, and I recall the memory of searching through the grass at family events, my fingers sticky with beer, dropping the caps into an empty shoebox.

"They weren't exactly clean," I say, throwing the cap into the river. I had all sorts of collections as a kid—rocks, coins, buttons. I liked things that fit in my pocket, that I could carry with me anywhere.

I lead May to the area behind the willows, hidden away from any passersby who wants to share in the river's beauty. Like a jealous lover, I shield the river to myself in this cutoff corner from the rest of the cement walkway. I lay out the blanket, and we sit closely together in my favorite spot.

"I think I'm going to apply to the community college nearby," I say, and May gives me a sideways look.

"That's probably a good idea." She offers a small smile.

"This way I can keep an eye on my mom and still move

forward." I turn on my side and stroke the side of May's cheek. She wiggles her nose at my touch.

"Standing still isn't a bad thing, darling."

"I know." I watch May close her eyes as a cloud unblocks the sun. "It feels like I've been in the same spot for a while now though, and it'd be nice to leave one day soon." The thought of experiencing something new, filled with strangers and foreign sights, sends a quick shiver through my bones. A mixture of anxiety and excitement.

"Leaving won't change this." May turns on her side so that she faces me and lays a gentle hand over my heart. I close my eyes and focus on the pounding for a moment. "Traveling brings enlightenment, but running away won't make anything different."

"What are you a fortune cookie now?" I look up at her and smirk.

"Has my advice been reduced to generic umbrella state-ments?" May turns on her back, and I tickle my hands up her side, making her squirm.

I grab May's hand. "What will change this?" She looks at me, and the corners of her lips twitch upward for a moment.

"It's a slow process." I sigh at her words, and we sit in silence, watching the clouds pass. "When we first met you couldn't look me in the eyes fully. When you smiled it looked as if it caused a tremendous strain on your cheeks." May cups my face. "I'd touch you, and I could feel a sting of memories too painful to talk about." I blush at May's words and look away. She sits up and hovers over me.

"You don't feel as heavy now. When you smile I know it's genuine, and when I touch you..." May grabs a handful of my hair and tugs gently. "You embrace it."

"I've always embraced your touches." I trace my fingers up May's arms.

"Perhaps part of you, but there was shame in your eyes in allowing me to care for you," May says softly.

"I wanted you too much." I squeeze my arms around May. "It felt shameful," I mumble into her.

"It's what you needed, darling." May kisses my head. I look down towards the willows and then back up at her.

"If I left...when I leave...I won't be running." I stare into May's eyes, and she kisses me on the lips. "You'll be with me, right?" I ask and kiss her back harder.

"Always." May smiles. I feel her fingers still in my hair and relax into her touch. I can hear the river's gentle movement, the wind carrying its own quiet melody. This is tranquility.

CHAPTER 17

MAY MEETS me by my locker, and we walk into Economics together, taking two seats in the back row. I'm feeling tired and focus on my sketchbook to keep myself from dozing off as Mr. Busman lectures. Eventually packets are passed around for us to work on, and I scoot my desk closer to May's.

"I love how your hair falls over your eyes while you're focusing," she whispers in my ear. I glance sideways and try not to smile.

"Autumn." Mr. Busman calls out as he hangs up the phone. My head shoots up and everyone turns and stares at me. "You're wanted in the principal's office." His eyes are soft, like a cloud blowing through a sunny day. The room is strangely quiet, and my face grows hot. Something bad has happened. Why else would the principal want to see me? May puts her hand over mine.

"It's going to be okay," she whispers, giving me a tilted smile. I nod to myself and pack up my things. Everyone continues to stare as I walk to the front of the room, even Mr. Busman. In the hallway, by myself, I feel like I can breathe again. I lean my back against the wall and try to stop my legs from shaking. I don't know why I'm overcome with such anxiety. There's probably nothing to worry about. The principal could want to see me for a number of reasons. I kick off the wall and pull my backpack tightly to my shoulders. My mother's been doing so well lately. She must be fine.

The main office is near the front entrance of the school. When I knock on the glass door the secretary waves me in.

"Autumn, right?" Her beady eyes squint down at me from the high raised desk. The wrinkles in her face fall forward like the cheeks of a bulldog and then draw back tightly as she awaits my response. I nod my head, confused by the way her eyes examine me. "Through there, honey." I follow her long, outstretched finger pointed to the principal's separate office and quickly turn away from her. I stop for a moment before the wooden door and then in one swift motion lift my sweaty palm up, twist the knob, and swing it open.

"Mom?" I notice her right away. Her dark hair is pulled into a tight bun, and her old red purse hangs off the edge of the chair. Her head snaps to the door like a rubber band pulled too tight. I immediately notice her swollen eyes and a gloss of snot beneath her nose. I want to step back out of the door, close it, and run, but she smiles sadly and tilts her head to her shoulder. Something about it makes me walk closer to her.

"Autumn, please, have a seat." Mr. Harris, the principal, stands next to his desk. He has a full head of thick, white hair that trails down his face and into a beard. I've never actually stood this close to him. He's at least a whole foot taller than me and is more than just a little intimidating. This is the first time he's ever had to say my name, and it's weird since we've never actually formally met. He instructs me to the seat next to my mother and sits down behind his own desk. I watch as he begins to fidget with the pencils, pens, and coffee cups scattered in front of him.

"What's going on?" I ask, turning to my mother. She quickly turns to Mr. Harris, who shoots his head up.

"We're just waiting for Mrs. Nelson to come back before we begin. She had to step out for a minute. How are you feeling today, Autumn?" Principal Harris interrupts the private conversation I want to have with my mother. I keep looking at her, waiting for a response.

"They called me a few weeks ago, but I ignored them because you seemed fine." She leans into me, almost whispering, her voice harsh from tears. "You kept telling me you had a new friend." She reaches out and grabs hold of my arm, squeezing it harder than I think she intended to.

"Is this about May and our relationship?" I look between my mother and Principal Harris. They say nothing. "I realize it may seem strange to you, but it's not a big deal. We love each other. Maybe I should've told you, but I didn't want to cause you any more stress." I grab hold of the hand clutching my arm and squeeze it. My mother has to understand the tightrope between sanity and lunacy that I've been walking with her.

"Does she go to school with you?" My mother asks slowly. Mr. Harris leans forward, his thick eyebrows pushed together like mountain slopes.

"Yeah, we have classes together," I reply. "Mom, if this is what this meeting is about, can we just go home and talk about it?" I don't want to be in the principal's office anymore. I can feel sweat crawl underneath my arms as the room gets hotter and hotter.

"Autumn, you've gone to this girl's house before. You've slept over for Christ's sake!" She flings her hands in the air in front of her, and I'm taken aback by the outburst. Mr. Harris clears his throat.

"Mom, it's okay." I put my hands on her shoulders and look into her eyes. "Please Mom, let me explain," I say desperately, but her body stays rigid. The door swings open and all three of us jump.

"Hello everyone, sorry that took so long." Mrs. Nelson walks in and pulls up a chair diagonal to mine. She sets a manila envelope on top of a stack of papers, and I read my name in cursive on the side of it.

"What's that?" I point to the file, and Mrs. Nelson puts her hand on it, keeping me from touching the folder.

"Autumn, how are you feeling today?" She smiles, red lipstick smeared on her teeth.

"Why is everyone asking me that? I'm fine. I just want to know what's going on. Why am I in trouble for being with May?" I try to control my voice, but I'm so angry no one's explained the reason for this awkward gathering. I'm close to yelling.

"Honey, no one here is saying that you're in trouble. We just want to talk to you." Mrs. Nelson pats my leg and pushes her glasses up on her nose. Her unwanted contact gives me the immature urge to spit at her, but I refrain.

"Why though? Why do we have to talk about me and May?" I move my legs away from her reach and straighten up. It's not fair that I'm being attacked three to one right now. I wish that someone was on my side.

"Well…" Mrs. Nelson looks back and forth between Mr. Harris and my mother. They wait for her to continue. "We're concerned that your relationship might be a little bit abnormal." The comment is like a slap in the face. My mother puts her hand on my shoulder, but I shove her off immediately.

"You've been spending all of your time with her, Autumn," my mother says. "I've never met her."

"You couldn't have." I clench my teeth, the heat becoming unbearable. I feel like I might pass out.

"Why wouldn't your mother have been able to meet May?" Mrs. Nelson steps in and pulls my focus to her god-awful makeup job.

"Because—" I pause for a moment and run my hands over my head. It feels heavy, like my brain is bloated, and I squint my eyelids shut, trying to focus. "There's always too much else going on." I look down at the floor and kick the dirty blue carpet. It's too hard to explain, and I feel betrayed that my mother even agreed to be part of a meeting like this. The anger inside of me rises, and I tighten my fists.

"Have I seen May before?" My mother asks, but I don't answer. I look at all of them staring at me. Mr. Harris seems slightly intrigued, his hands folded underneath his chin, but I can hear his foot tapping to some off-rhythm. Mrs. Nelson scribbles everything down in the file. My mother's shoulders are slumped forward, not quite in defeat, but definitely worn out, tired. I want to shake her, to force her eyes open, but I also want to crawl up next to her and shut the world away. It's too much to handle.

"I don't have to take part in this." I stand up and lift my backpack over my shoulders.

"Autumn, please, you have to try." My mother jumps in front of me and leads me back into my seat.

"May knows everything. I've told her all about you. All about our fucked up family." I stand up so that I'm a half-inch shy of staring my mother straight in the eyes.

"Is May always there for you to confide in?" Mrs. Nelson asks, nodding slowly, as if she's hoping for me to continue. I shake my head and take a step forward.

"I don't agree with this. I don't know these people." I wave my hand in front of Mrs. Nelson and Principal Harris. "If you wanted to talk to me, you should've done so at home." I shove past my mother, but she grabs my arm.

"I didn't know, Autumn." My mother gently pulls me back, like she's reeling in a fish. I'm shocked by her softness. "I didn't know you needed this much help."

Her words whirl in a tornado of hazy auburn in my head; I'm confused and angered. My lip spasms, and the heat of panic sends tears to dance along the margin of my eyelids. I step out of her reach and pull my arm away.

"I'm done with this. I'm done doing what you want, and I'm done taking care of you." I push her arm to the side and step past her. Mr. Harris stands up from his chair, cautiously, as if he's watching a car accident in slow motion. "I've been nothing but supportive of you, but I guess that doesn't matter, does it? This is why Dad won't come back," I mumble the last part, and take another step forward. The air is stale and quiet, but Mrs. Nelson coughs uncomfortably and starts rummaging through my file.

My mother puts her hand up to her mouth.

"What do you mean by that?" she asks, and I turn around because her voice sounds raspy. The bones in her jaw quiver in a gentle hum like the strings of a cello. The fire in my chest immediately burns with a swift rain of guilt.

"I'm sorry, I didn't mean that. I'm just upset." I struggle to find the words to apologize, but my throat is dry, and everyone is staring at me.

"Shit, I'm sorry," I exclaim, my hands outstretched.

"Autumn, what happened to your father isn't your mother's fault," Mrs. Nelson says finally. The statement hangs in the air as if there's more to follow. She looks towards Principal Harris who immediately throws his head down and stares at the floor. Then she looks at my mother who's still staring directly at me.

"What do you think happened to your father?" My mom steps closer to me, and I think she might want to touch me, but she looks afraid, like I might suddenly disappear.

"What do you mean? He left. He walked out on us. He told me that you guys were having too many problems, and he couldn't live in the house anymore." I recall his words in my ear, his voice raspy, and hopeless.

"When did he tell you that?" Mrs. Nelson interrupts while thumbing through my file again.

"I don't know, like October." I take a step closer to her, wanting to see what she's looking for.

"How did he tell you that?" My mother asks, softly.

"Over the phone." I don't understand the questions. "Is he missing or something?" I start to worry. It's been over a month since we've last talked, and I immediately feel bad for not keeping up with him.

"No, he's not missing, Autumn." Mrs. Nelson pulls a paper forward and skims over it. I watch as her mouth slowly drops open. "Your father's been dead for almost a year." She looks up at me, astonished, and I feel faint.

"What?" The air in the room becomes too thick to swallow. I try to breathe in, but nothing is enough. I put my hands on top of my knees and hear my mother's voice—a faraway sound—say something soothing as she rubs my back. I bolt upright, stumble towards Mrs. Nelson, and grab the file out of her hand. My mother takes hold of my wrist immediately.

"Autumn, your dad shot himself in the head six months after Mya died." Her nails dig into my wrist, and I drop the file on the floor. "I'm sorry, honey." She grabs me behind the neck and pulls me into an embrace. "I had no idea that you —" Her tears fall down my neck and start to wet the collar of my shirt. My head is spinning, and I have no choice but to lean into her.

"There's no easy way to tell you this, dear." Mrs. Nelson's hand touches my shoulder. "But we think that because of all the stress you've been going through you may be imagining figures to help." I push away from everyone.

"Help?" I wipe away the wetness.

"Help you cope." Mrs. Nelson puts her hands together and offers a small smile, laid heavily with accomplishment, as if she just solved the world's greatest mystery.

"You don't think that May is real?" I ask, not believing my own words. Mrs. Nelson nods immediately, but I look over at my mom, who first stares at the floor, but then manages to meet my gaze. "You think that I've imagined her?" I ask more aggressively.

"We don't have any record of her in our school system," Principal Harris says, finally finding his voice in the conversation.

"I've been to her house before. I've met her mother. She's real!"

"Where does she live?" Mr. Harris asks in such a calm way that I think he must be mocking me.

"38 Maple Avenue." I try to keep my mind—which feels like it's been filled with cement—focused as I watch the three of them look between each other. My mother puts a knuckle in her mouth and squints her eyebrows together.

"I'm pretty sure that's one of the houses in disrepair," Principal Harris mumbles. "I live a few streets away," he adds, and Mrs. Nelson feigns interest, but my mother looks at me through puddles. Her mouth falls open. It's too hard to stay put. I move quickly past her, swing open every single door keeping me inside the building, and run.

CHAPTER 18

My legs take me to the river. I hide behind the willows and dig my nails into my hair, trying to make sense of what just happened. The world spins, and it feels like I'm falling. I stand up and look down into the water. It's probably cold enough to send my body into a state of shock. It could at least wake me up.

"Autumn." The voice behind me sucks all the air from my lungs. I turn around slowly and see May, not even a foot away. I look her up and down, but I'm too afraid to reach out and touch her.

"You're not real," I whisper, and my voice cracks. The corners of her lips dip downward, but she doesn't break eye contact. "I need you." I pound the palm of my fist into my chest. I close my eyes and see her behind my eyelids.

"You can't leave me," I mumble, keeping my eyes closed. "I can't stand the thought of being old one day, sitting at a table in a kitchen that doesn't feel like my own, and kissing lips that don't belong to you." I reach out my hand and imagine cupping her cheek. "I'm going to wonder what transpired in my life, how I could've allowed this to happen. Not when I was once so close to being happy." The only sound I hear in response is the river hitting shore. My lips uncontrollably tremble, and I open my eyes slowly, as if they'd been nailed shut for a very long time. It's empty in front of me. Screams echo inside my chest, and I lift my hand over my mouth to keep them inside.

"Autumn." I whip my head towards the sound of my name. My mother's in the distance, waving at me. My cheeks grow hot, and I don't know how to face her. I sit back down, but the willows don't shield her entrance. She breathes heavily, and the tip of her nose is red. She sits next to me and it feels strange sharing my secret space with her.

"How did you find me?" I ask, my eyes set on the water. She exhales forcibly.

"To be honest, it was a lucky guess." She shrugs, but then adds, "You and Mya used to walk here together." I feel her inch closer to me. We sit in silence and watch the water drift about in heavy waves.

"Your father was a very loving man," my mom says, letting out a long sigh, like she'd been holding something inside of her for a long time. "And he was incredibly strong. I don't even know how he did it." She throws her hands up in the air. "The years Mya was sick were so traumatic. There was just so much suffering. We had to watch, helplessly, as our daughter painfully struggled to survive for so long. It changed us." I keep my hands busy by playing with the rocks on the ground, but my ears are ringing. "I was told he was drunk when he did it. I like to imagine that if he'd waited until he sobered he wouldn't have, but I'm not sure that would've even mattered." She laughs slightly, and her shoulders fall. She looks at me, and our eyes meet.

"I thought about killing myself so many times, Autumn." She pauses, and a stray tear trickles halfway down her cheek before she quickly wipes it away. Her lips start to quiver. "I'd think of you though. I'd remember you, and I couldn't do it. I couldn't leave you, and I think I resented you for that." My mom puts her hand on my arm. "I'm sorry, Autumn."

The touch makes me shiver. It's hard and real, and I close my eyes, sinking my head into my knees. I try to intake air, but every time I breathe in there's not enough. I feel fingers run through my hair, a soothing voice whisper in my ear, and I can't help the sobs that follow.

"No one was there for me," I say, and the wind mimics the twisting hole drilling in my stomach. "It was so lonely." Everything inside of me breaks down, like a castle crumbling. I can feel my walls crushing into dust. My mom puts her arm around me, and I lean into her lap and sob. I close my eyes, and time transpires without me. I hold onto my mother's legs like they're my boat, and I'm drifting in the river.

"I don't want to lose her," I mumble into my mom's jeans. Her fingers run through my hair, and she waits, probably at a loss for words.

"I don't think you'll ever lose her," she says slowly. I sit up and turn so that I'm facing her. She wipes the tears from my face with her shirt sleeve. "Technically, she'll always be inside of you." She smiles and touches her pointer finger to my head. I scuff at the joke.

"I know, I'm crazy." I wipe the remaining tears from my face and shake my head.

"It's been a rough few years." My mom peels the wet strands of hair away from my forehead. "We're going to get you help." She rubs my shoulders with both of her hands and flashes a small smile. "We're going to figure this out togeth-er." I immediately remember a similar exchange of words between my mom and Mya on a hospital bed. I lean away, feeling as though I'm going to hurl.

"I'm sorry," I stutter. My mom grabs my chin and forces me to look at her.

"You have nothing to apologize for," she says with so much authority in her voice I believe her.

When we make it back to our house my mom makes me tea, and we sit on the couch together. I feel hollow and drained, but I rest my head on my mother's shoulder and it seems like enough.

"What am I going to do about school?" There's only a few weeks left. I couldn't bear the thought of doing the whole year over again when I'm so close to finishing.

"You'll probably be able to finish everything remotely." My mom pats my knee.

"Where am I going to go?" I try to ignore the tremor in my voice.

"Why do you think you're going to go somewhere?" She asks, her words slow.

"I'm crazy. Aren't they going to make you lock me up?" I close my eyes and a few remaining tears drip out.

"I'd never let anyone take you, Autumn." She shifts so that she's staring into my eyes. "You just need some help. I'll find you someone to talk to." She grabs my shoulders and holds me against her chest.

"I need you," I say into her, and she holds me tighter. "I need you to care about me, I need you to love me, and I need you to actually be there for me." I choke out the words as quickly as my tongue allows. I feel her nodding her head against me.

"I promise, Autumn. I'm here now." I wrap my arms

around her waist and allow her to rub my back as I relax into her. The past few hours feel like a dream. I struggle to keep my eyelids open, but the fight doesn't last long, and I welcome the darkness that finally allows peace.

CHAPTER 19

I WAKE up but keep my eyes closed, letting my head sink further into the pillow. I try to enjoy the comfort of sleep a few moments longer and bunch the blankets underneath my arm, clutching the bundle against my chest. It feels good for a moment, to keep my eyes closed and pretend that she's still here with me. I'm not supposed to indulge these thoughts, but it doesn't matter. The truth has taken away the ecstasy of our relationship, and honestly, the thought of seeing her again terrifies me. I open my eyes slowly and let go of the blanket.

It's late in the morning, almost noon, and there's a note on the kitchen table from my mom saying she's gone grocery shopping. I look outside the window and see the sun shining through the blinds. I imagine the warmth on my skin and stumble outside to the tire swing. The earth is alive and well, and I try to find comfort in the noise of trees and birds. I breathe in and lean my chest against the rope. The past few weeks have gone by quickly, even though I haven't gone to school.

I hear a door open and close and look out to see Jamie

walking across his lawn over to me. We make eye contact, and he waves with a sideways smile.

"Does this mean that you're finally done?" I call out.

"The graduation ceremony is on Friday." He stands in front of me and hides his hands in his jean pockets. "You going?"

I shake my head. It was a tough choice. I wasn't sure if I'd be letting my mom down or not, but she never brought it up, and I was thankful for that.

"It'll probably be pretty boring anyway. Lots of crying. Too much drama." I smile up at him.

"I should've come over sooner," he says, his voice harsh and quiet.

"You didn't know."

"I did, Autumn." The words rush out of his mouth like a balloon popping. "I heard the rumors, that you were talking to yourself. I was just scared. After Mya died, it was easier to distance myself from you and ignore it all. I couldn't face it." He puts his hands behind his head and lifts his eyebrows. "I shouldn't have done that."

"It's okay." I swing forward slightly and touch his arm. "I haven't exactly been facing it either." We smile at each other.

"How are you?" he asks, and I roll my eyes.

"That's a challenging question." I cock my eyebrow up at him.

"I'm sorry," he stammers, but I cut him off.

"I miss her." I nod my head and look up at him. "And I know that's crazy, but it was nice having someone who understood everything I went through." I look down at my shoes kicking up small dusts of dirt below the swing. Jamie grabs the rope right above where my hands hold on and pulls it towards him.

"There's a lucky girl out there who'll be willing to put in

a lot of effort to learn everything about you, and she'll fall in love with you, and it'll feel amazing." Jamie's eyes shine as they light up, and I smile at his kind words.

"I don't think I'm ready for all that yet." Jamie lets go of the rope, and I swing backwards. I rock back and forth a few times, and Jamie stares up at the branch, perhaps trying to examine his old knot from the ground.

"Do you have any ideas of what you might do?" he asks, diverting his eyes as he waits for a response.

"I think maybe there's something out there I don't know about, some way I can actually make a difference in the world. So far my life has been spent in a box. There has to be something more."

"Is that healthy?" Jamie asks, his voice pitched in an attempt to sound relaxed, but I can see the concern glistening in the beads of sweat dripping along his forehead.

"In an untraditional sense, I think the answer is yes." I pause for a moment and think of May, how her smile would calm me. "There was so much pain for so long, taking up all the space around me, inside of me." I look up at Jamie. "I want to help other people with that pain."

I kick my feet off the ground and lean back in the swing so that I'm looking up at the sky. Suddenly, the rope tugs forward and the tire sinks downward. I look up to see Jamie standing on the tire, his hands holding the rope slightly above mine. I smile at the familiarity.

"What do you have in mind?" He watches as the branch dips down with the extra weight and steps off the swing, still holding onto the rope.

"I want to give back to the community in some way. I'm not sure how yet, but my mom says that once I'm done with therapy we can do it together."

"That sounds like a really good plan." Jamie smiles and

nods his head. "You'll have to make time to visit me in college.'

"I'd love that." I think of the river and all the old houses, the hidden places of beauty worth searching for, and realize I'm not ready to leave this town yet.

"It'll be fun." Jamie looks around and puts his hands on his hips. "Enjoy your day, Autumn."

"You too." I climb out of the tire swing and give him a hug. He wraps his lanky arms around me and squeezes so hard my feet lift off the ground. I watch him turn and walk back to his own porch. He waves once more before going inside. It's a nice day. I think I'll walk down to the river later and skip some stones, maybe mow the lawn.

I walk inside and go upstairs to the bathroom. I turn the hot water on and begin to take off my clothes. The sun shines through the curtains, and I notice the old pencil trace of leaves on the wall. They're slightly out of place now. A bit higher than they were before. I touch them with my fingers. The pencil I originally used is still on the counter ledge. I trace the new leaves and write the date next to them.

My back tenses when the hot water hits, and I knead my muscles as I rotate my shoulders. I press slowly but hard, working my way down. I take the shower extension and bring it closer so that it's pointed directly in between my shoulder blade and neck. My mouth falls open in pleasure, and I switch shoulders. I trail the water down slowly, hitting my chest and abdomen. I spread myself open and feel the water pound warm pellets that land like a sheet spread above a bed inside me. I close my eyes and grasp at the pleasure, holding it until it escalades into a warm erosion. I settle into the feeling and then it slowly disappears. I finish showering and wrap a towel around my hair so that it doesn't drip on the carpet on the way to my room.

I sit on my bed to dry off and feel something poke at my thigh. I look down and notice the corner of a photo sticking out. I pull it to the light but already know it's the picture of Mya after the transplant. I lay it on my bed and start to get dressed. It's been awhile since I saw a picture of my sister's face, and I smile down at it while stuffing my legs into a pair of jeans. I take the photo and hop down the stairs into the living room. I walk over to the bookshelf and shove my hand behind it. I'd forgotten about the photo album. I pull it out and shake off the dust gathered in bunches along its cover.

The house is quiet and peaceful. I sit on the couch and open the album on my lap. I flip through the photos and start to remember memories long forgotten. Birthday parties, visits to the beach, apple picking—all the times we enjoyed life together. When I get to the end I pull back the plastic screen and place the picture of Mya behind it. I touch it one more time before closing the album and setting it on the coffee table. I lean back into the couch and wait. Maybe when my mom comes home we'll take a walk to the river.

ABOUT THE AUTHOR

KD Rye spent her youth day dreaming and reading comic books. She holds a bachelor's degree in creative writing, a Juris Doctorate, and a Masters in Business Administration. She enjoys conversation via bar top and playing rugby. If you meet her in person she will probably challenge you to an arm wrestling match…and you will probably lose.

Sign up for her mailing list and stay up to date on all writing news at kdrye.com.

ALSO BY KD RYE

Women in Gray

Henry's Departure